Silent Hearts

Cameron D. James

Winnipeg, Canada

Published May 2018 by Deep Desires Press
an imprint of Story Perfect Inc.

Deep Desires Press
PO Box 51053 Tyndall Park
Winnipeg, Manitoba R2X 3B0
Canada

Visit http://www.deepdesirespress.com for more scorching hot erotica and erotic romance.

WIN FREE BOOKS!
Subscribe to our email newsletter to get notified of all our hot new releases, sales, and giveaways! Visit deepdesirespress.com/newsletter to sign up today!

Silent Hearts

Chapter One

Saturday, 2:13 AM

JAKE HATED THIS SONG, BUT THEY played it so much it was lodged in his brain. He mumbled the lyrics and bobbed his head as he dug his hands deep into the scone mix, the metal bowl clattering on the counter.

The hostel was quiet, as it always was during his graveyard shift. He liked the silence, preferring it over the busyness of the day shift. He liked his solitude. Eleven at night to seven in the morning without a single interruption, except if a drunk stumbled back late, but they tended to pass out quickly. Plus, this shift meant he got a scone fresh out of the oven.

The door behind him clicked as it opened. "I hate this song," Jake muttered, distinctly and loudly enough for his visitor to hear. He put his focus entirely on mixing the dough—the more nonchalant his comment sounded, the more believable it would be.

When the person behind him didn't say anything, Jake turned around. "I'm sorry, but the kitchen is closed until morning."

Jake stumbled over his last few words as he saw his visitor. The man was in his early twenties and beefy...and nearly naked. Jake felt his cock stir. It took a moment for his brain to shift back into coherent functioning. This had to be one of the men he passed in the lobby earlier, one of the Russians that arrived this evening. Whatever possessed a Russian wrestling team to tour rural Scotland, Jake would never know.

The man was tall and blond, his arms and chest bulging with hard muscle. His chest was shaved smooth and his nipples stood out like pink dimes. And he stood just inside the kitchen door wearing nothing but a loose fitting pair of boxers. If the bulge was any indication, this Russian was packing some serious meat.

Jake felt his face warm with a flush. He turned to the sink to rinse his hands, then cleared his throat and tried again. "The kitchen is closed until seven. If you need water, you can get a drink from the bathroom."

It was clear from the Russian's eyes that he didn't understand the statement. The man lifted his fist and pointed. "You...Jake?" Each word was an effort.

He didn't know if he should be terrified or curious. Jake nodded.

The Russian dropped his pointing hand to his crotch and grabbed his cock through the thin boxers. "You…suck."

Jake's mouth twitched and a smile tugged at the corner of his mouth. "Now you're speaking my language."

He tossed the dishtowel on the counter and fell to his knees before the Russian hunk. Jake tugged the man's pale blue boxers down and a large, semi-hard cock flopped out. It was uncut, fully shaved, and smooth. Dangling between his legs was a pair of low hangers, the size of plum tomatoes, as smooth as his dick.

A glistening, crystal-clear drop of precum lazily pooled at the tip and began its slow descent to the ground. Jake caught it with his finger and brought it to his lips, rubbing the sweet fluid over his mouth and then licking it off. A thin strand of precum linked his lips with the Russian's cock.

Jake looked up at the man, flashing a hungry grin. The Russian sneered. "Suck."

Without hesitation, Jake slid the cock past his lips and deep into his mouth. It tasted of sweat and unwashed skin. He gripped the man's dick in his fist and slid it luxuriously out of his mouth. Jake licked every inch of skin, savoring the taste that went along with the man-stink that drove him wild.

Even fully hard, the man's foreskin wreathed his head in a thick wrinkle of skin. Jake suckled the skin, pulling it into his mouth. He gently gripped it with his lips and tongue, stretching it. With a few deft maneuvers of his mouth, Jake slid the tip of his tongue between the head of his cock and foreskin. He teased the extra skin—nibbling, stretching, licking.

He then launched into full suck-mode, pressing tightly with his lips and bobbing his head at a ferocious speed. He closed his eyes, allowing his senses of touch, taste, and smell to take over. While his right hand held the cock steady and in place, his left hand fondled the man's balls. They were impeccably smooth to the touch, probably shaved mere hours before. Jake massaged each testicle, giving them gentle tugs with each press of his fingers.

The bulky man groaned and muttered in Russian, words Jake didn't know. The tone, the breathlessness, and the urgency, though, told him everything. Two strong hands held the sides of Jake's head, holding him in place. The Russian pumped his hips back and forth, fucking Jake's mouth.

He suppressed a gagging cough that threatened to interrupt when the shaved dick hit the back of his throat. A little discomfort was worth it.

Jake tilted his head to watch the Russian's face as he shoved his powerful cock in his mouth. The man's eyes were screwed shut and his face was flushed.

The moment was soon. Jake smiled around the thick cock in the way of his lips. His fingers moved from the man's balls to his taint, massaging the patch of skin. It was doing something; a new charge pulsed through the man's thrusting.

The man's whole body tensed and he exclaimed something in Russian that Jake took to mean, "I'm coming!"

Jake closed his eyes and tried to shut out all senses except taste. Warm, sticky cum filled his mouth with its slightly-salty taste. After swallowing it, another long burst filled his mouth again. He downed the second mouthful and opened his eyes, slowly returning to his other senses.

The Russian's hands loosened their grip and his breath came in heavy pants. He carefully pulled his limp dick from Jake's mouth. "*Pasib.*"

"You're welcome," Jake said, tugging the man's boxers back up. A moment later, Jake was alone. He washed his hands and returned to mixing the dough for the scones.

That was the seventh guy to ask for a blowjob in the past two weeks. This hostel was part of a chain that operated through much of Scotland, and a lot of tour busses and independent travelers took advantage of the prime location and low prices, with many travelling a circuit through the chain's hostels across the country. Word had apparently travelled through the chain about the Canadian who gave midnight blowjobs in Kyleakin.

Jake portioned out the dough on a set of baking sheets and popped them in the oven. As he waited for them to bake, he reached over to the radio and changed the stations, quickly finding that same crappy pop song on another frequency. Leaning against the counter, he hummed along.

Saturday, 3:02 PM

Jake ran his fingers through his wet hair and yawned, descending the steps from the staff dorm in the attic. His stomach growled loudly. On graveyard shift hours, this was breakfast time.

"Afternoon, Audra," Jake said as he passed the front desk. The woman waved absently at him, immersed in a video of some sort on the company laptop.

He cringed as he approached the kitchen; the door was closed and already his ears were assaulted with noise. Jake entered and paused.

The kitchen was full of Russians. The decibel level hurt his ears and he couldn't understand a word of it. Squeezing through the crowd of muscular men toward the fridge, he prayed he didn't pop a boner and accidentally brush up against the wrong man. Half the men were butt-ugly, though, so it reduced his boner risk considerably. He stood at only half-chubby.

Opening the fridge, he found his loaf of bread—with his name clearly written across the bag—half missing. He pulled it out and eyed the horde of Russians. A lot of them were eating bread with a dark spread. Exasperated, Jake dug his jar of Nutella out of the cupboard, also with his name written across it. Most of it had disappeared since he'd last opened it.

Jake glared at the backs of the Russians. His deadly stare fell upon a familiar face purposely ignoring him—last night's hookup. Jake's ire softened, but it didn't disappear.

Turning back to the counter, Jake dug two slices out of the bag and popped them in the toaster. He watched the appliance do its work. It was boring, but he didn't want to stare at the hunk from last night or any of his friends. It might make the guy uncomfortable...or maybe make Jake hard at exactly the wrong time.

Behind him, the voices faded as the group migrated elsewhere. Jake hung his head until the toaster *chunked* and popped his breakfast up. He grabbed one of the plates piled next to the toaster and slathered what was left of his Nutella onto his toast. He tossed the knife in the sink to wash after eating and groaned at the pile of unwashed dishes left behind by the Russians. When Jake put the jar back in the cupboard, he shoved it behind someone else's jam.

"Excuse me," a voice behind him said, deep and masculine.

Jake jolted. He had thought he was alone.

The guy behind him looked like he'd stepped off the cover of a highland romance novel or something. He was tall, broad shouldered, and exuded masculinity. His fitted, white, button up shirt hung amazingly on his frame, tightening against all the right bulges. The man wore a kilt on his lower half, sporran unfortunately covering his crotch, and his very hairy and muscled legs stood below.

"Um…pardon?"

"The toaster," the man said, pointing behind Jake. "I'd like to toast some bread."

Jake couldn't help but stare. His blue eyes and dirty blond hair contrasted against the dark stubble of a few days' growth.

"I'd, uh, like to make a sandwich and want to toast my bread first," the man said, when Jake didn't move or respond. He enunciated each word carefully, seemingly unsure if Jake spoke English.

"Oh, of course, of course." Jake moved aside. "I'm sorry. I just woke up, I'm not quite with it yet."

"No problem, mate." The Scot opened the fridge and leaned down to search for his things. His kilt draped over the astounding curve of his ass, rising in the back, almost, but not quite, giving Jake a glance of the goods.

Jake tilted his head to the side, without thought, gaze rolling down the man's lines. He caught himself and righted his head before he stood upright and turned around. Jake leaned against the counter, trying to appear nonchalant.

"Party late last night?" the man said. That accent made everything sexy. Jake wished he could wrap it around himself like a blanket.

"No, I'm on staff here. Graveyard shift."

The Scot smiled, adorable dimples sprouting on his cheeks. "Ah, nice. I just arrived a couple hours ago; I'm here for a week."

"Cool. My name's Jake Coleman, by the way." The Scot's eyes widened almost imperceptibly. Had he heard of him already? He stuck out his hand.

"I'm Grant MacLean."

Jake could feel a blush coming to his cheeks, so he let go of Grant's hand before it could bloom into full redness sprawled across his face.

"If you ever need anything...especially at night...let me know." Jake fought to keep any seductiveness out of his voice, but still lowered his face and looked out the tops of his eyes. He had to be careful. While he wanted to know what this guy had under his kilt, he didn't want to get punched out if the man was straight.

Grant put a couple slices in the toaster and pushed the lever. "You're not from around here, are you?"

"No, I'm from Canada."

"Canada? *Due South*! I loved that show!"

Jake rolled his eyes. Something like half the locals had told him that at one point or another. He'd never seen the show himself.

Grant arched an eyebrow. "Long way to come for some crappy job."

Jake smirked. "Yeah, I'm from Grayson, Saskatchewan—it's like the middle of nowhere." He shoved his toast in his mouth and tore off a bite. A mouthful of food prevented him from getting into another rant about how much his hometown sucked. After he chewed and swallowed, he added, "I came here for a two-

month vacation and ended up getting a work visa. I've
been at this hostel ever since."

"Nice. How long ago was that?" Grant crossed his
arms and leaned his hip against the counter, next to Jake.
Casual, comfortable, masculine, and dead-sexy with those
legs. He stood so close to Jake he could feel the heat
emanating off his body. Something that felt like static
electricity pulsed in the small space between them. Jake
wondered if Grant felt it too.

"About ten months ago. I need to decide soon if I
want to go home or apply to stay another year."

When Grant's toast popped up, he dug through the
fridge for a few of his ingredients, giving Jake another
glimpse of the man's glorious ass.

"And what are you leaning toward?"

"Huh?" *That ass...*

"Your decision. Stay here or go home?"

Jake chewed on another sweet mouthful of toast,
anything to distract him from the man's round cheeks and
the kilt gracefully draped over them. "To be honest, I don't
know. I kind of feel like I'm getting nowhere here—I'm
stuck in a rut of working and sleeping, with not much else.
But home isn't all that different. I'd be going to the same
nowhere, just as fast."

"Yeah?"

"You're from around here, right?" Jake steered their
conversation away from his home life.

Grant paused in his sandwich making to look at him for a moment, then let it slide. "I live in Edinburgh, but I'm from Pitlochry. I graduated last year and do IT stuff at a tech company."

"Cool. Totally opposite of my skill set." Jake finished off the last of his toast, licking the bits of Nutella off his fingers, and slid them in and out of his mouth slowly, seductively.

Grant watched Jake's fingers for a moment. "Oh, yeah?" It might have been Jake's imagination, but there was a quiver in Grant's voice, a momentary weakness, a catch of breath.

"I studied music in university—graduated last year, too. Music and creative writing. I'm all arts—I can barely work a computer."

When Jake put his plate by the sink, his face fell at the sight of the other dishes from the Russians. By all rights, he should leave them there; it wasn't his mess and he wasn't working right now. Instead, he filled the sink and started washing. It would give him an excuse to stay in the kitchen and spend a couple more minutes with Grant.

"Well, we're evenly matched then. I don't have a creative bone in my body."

Jake smiled. *I'd like to put my creative bone in your body.* "You should come by the pub on Friday. I usually play a bit of piano there."

"Sure, that sounds good. Which pub?"

Jake snorted. "There's only two pubs around here and I don't think either one was a name. I'm pretty sure both signs just say 'Pub'."

Grant chuckled. "That's small town life for you." He put his condiments back in the fridge and picked up his sandwich. "Well, if you'll excuse me, I promised my sister I'd call her when I settled in. I'll get the pub details from you later."

"No problem, Grant. I'll see you around." And before the man could leave the kitchen, he added, "Remember, if you need anything at midnight, I'm right here."

Grant grunted something around the sandwich in his mouth and left. Jake smiled as he washed and dried the dishes. With any luck, he'd have his head underneath that kilt tonight.

Saturday, 7:17 PM

Jake leaned against the wall behind him. His cot squeaked with every movement he made. Aching for distraction, he got up and switched on the light, then sat down again and opened his notebook.

He rapped the pen against the pages as he caught sight of a gull just outside the miniscule window. It hovered in the air, catching updrafts, soaring in a long arc before flapping to gain altitude. Jake exhaled slowly and looked down at the page. It was empty. Still.

Jake carefully placed the nib on the paper, willing his hand to move, but too scared to follow through.

Finally, he slowly wrote *Dear Peter*. Scratching it out, he scrawled *Hi Peter* underneath. He stroked that out too.

Too casual, Jake thought, *but "Dear" is too…I don't know…too close.*

He could figure out the greeting later. *You're probably wondering why I'm writing a letter by hand, as I know we're both online almost every day.*

Jake skipped a couple lines and started again. *How've you been? I hope you're well.*

"That's a lame opener," Jake muttered and crossed it out. He closed his notebook, deciding to type it out and email it to him instead. Then he could fiddle with it.

He shook his head and opened the notebook again. An email was too impersonal. He brought the nib to the paper again and…did nothing. He'd wanted to write to Peter for the past ten months, to let it all out. But in ten months, he still hadn't figured out the first line.

He closed his notebook for a final time and shoved it under his pillow. He ran his fingers through his hair and stretched his back against the wall. *Maybe some piano would do the trick. Loosen me up, get my…feelings going…or something.*

Jake wandered through the village and entered his usual pub. The noise and clamor of drunken tourists assaulted his ears, most of them Russian. *Not going to work.* Jake turned around and walked back to the hostel, deciding to sit around and do nothing until his shift started.

Chapter Two

THE SAME CRAPPY SONG WAS ON THE radio again as Jake stirred muffin batter. Almost as if it were a repeat of the night before, the door behind him opened and someone entered.

"So you decided you need some after-midnight help?" Jake turned around and tried not to let his disappointment show. Rather than a hot Scotsman, standing just inside the kitchen door was a slightly-greasy bear of a man, maybe in his early thirties. He wore a drab green T-shirt riddled with heavy wrinkles and basketball shorts that hung down past his knees.

"Sorry," Jake said as he leaned over the sink to wash his hands. "I thought you were someone else. Is there something I can help you with?"

"Are you...are you Jake?" His voice was timid and shaky.

Jake tried valiantly to keep his face expressionless. "Yes. Do you need a hand with something?"

The man's face flushed and he averted his eyes. "I heard back in Oban about...well, about...I mean, I heard you..."

Jake wanted nothing more than to rub his eyes in exasperation, but he never turned down the opportunity to suck dick. Even if it was this guy. *Still, if I had a choice of who to suck...Grant...*

The man stuttered and mumbled his way through his words.

"Just say it already."

The man took a deep breath, his face bright red. "Will you suck me?" Then he blinked and looked away. "I'm sorry. You don't want to, I know. I'm sorry to bother you. I'll just go. I'll just—"

Jake reached out and grabbed the man's elbow. "If you promise to stop babbling, I'll suck you."

"Thank you. I mean, you don't have to. I don't usually do this sort of thing, but I—" Jake put his finger to his lips and shushed. The man clamped his mouth shut as Jake knelt on the floor and tugged the basketball shorts down. He paused at the athletic jockstrap underneath, but quickly pulled that down too. His bush was thick, but his dick was hard and a rather decent size. *Perhaps this won't be so bad after all.*

The man's cock had a wonderful mixture of firmness and softness. His dick was cut and his sac pulled tight against his body. Closing his eyes, Jake took the man in his mouth, sliding his lips up and down the length of the shaft.

His forehead repeatedly struck the man's belly. Thankfully, the man grabbed his stomach and lifted it out of the way. Jake pulled his mouth off the dick and looked at it. It glistened with saliva and it looked a lot bigger without the stomach overhang.

The man stood stock still and utterly silent as Jake first licked his balls and then stuffed his dick back in his mouth. He tightened the grip of his lips and created suction in his mouth. It was a move that brought quivers to the knees of many men. Yet this guy remained still as a statue. And whereas any man he'd serviced was moaning loudly at this point—often too loud—Jake couldn't even hear the man breathing over the faint music from the radio in the corner.

He worked up a rhythm, stroking his hand in front of his lips. There was the slightest tremor in the man's body. If Jake had to guess, the man was about to come.

The door behind them rattled and opened.

The man pulled up his shorts, but they got caught halfway up because his jockstrap refused to slide up his thighs. He whimpered and shuffled around the island in the middle of the room.

Jake leapt to his feet as the door opened fully. An older man, perhaps in his late fifties, dressed in only pajama pants, entered. He was a delicious-looking daddy-type. He eyed Jake up and down and then at the man on the other side of the island, who was beet red and still struggling with his shorts.

The man smiled. He had a caring face and a mess of black and gray hair carpeting his trim chest and stomach. "You must be Jake."

The fat man stopped struggling with his shorts and jockstrap, watching curiously.

"I am. You're looking for me?" Jake always felt the need to make the other guy explicitly state what he wanted. Making too many assumptions could lead to carelessness. He was a cockslut, yes, but a careful cockslut.

"I am." He glanced at the other man. "I'm here for the same reason he's here."

"Um, okay. I need to finish with him, though." Jake pointed over his shoulder with his thumb. *First time I've had a waiting list...*

"Of course."

More than a little stunned at how his shift was playing out, Jake reached for the bear's cock as he shuffled back toward Jake. Keeping his eyes on the older man, Jake took the fat man in his mouth and quickly worked up the same rhythm and intensity of before. Unfortunately, in the terror of being almost caught, the man's erection had gone to half-mast, so Jake had to firm him up to full strength. He closed his eyes and got fully into the action.

A few minutes into it, after the cock in his mouth was rock hard again, he felt a firm hand on his shoulder. Jake knew it had to be the older man as the bear was still holing his stomach out of the way.

Jake blindly reached out and found the man's leg. The pajama pants were soft, maybe even silk. He groped his way up the man's leg, fondling his crotch. From what Jake could tell, the man wasn't wearing any underwear and his cock was thick. *Very* thick.

The firm hand on his shoulder moved to his head, fingers running through his bristly hair. The thick dick behind the pajama pants thickened more as he groped it, but it didn't harden.

The bear shuddered again. He was close. Though there was no other outward sign of it, Jake knew. He'd sucked a lot of dick and he knew the signs, even on a guy as stolid as this.

A moment later, his mouth filled with warm and surprisingly sweet cum. "Mmm…"

The man let out a shuddering gasp that shook his body once more. Jake gently slid his mouth off his cock and licked it clean, sending another shiver through the man's frame.

Jake looked up at the man and winked. His face was no longer red as a stop sign; he seemed relaxed for the first time since he'd come in the kitchen. Jake tugged the man's jockstrap up and back into place, then helped him with the shorts.

"Can I watch you do him?" he whispered.

Jake looked at the older man's kind face. The man nodded. There was a twinkle in his eye.

Shifting over a foot, Jake pulled the man's pajamas down to find a cock that was as thick as he'd thought. It was cut and darker than the rest of the man's skin. A leather cock ring hugged around the base of the cock and balls. Precum collected at the tip.

Jake gripped the man's cock and gave it a couple firm tugs. It didn't harden. Mentally shrugging, he dragged his tongue across the man's slit, collecting the clear and tasty precum.

As he took the man in his mouth, his fingers ran over the leather cock ring and low-hanging sack. He hesitated when his fingers brushed across his taint and felt something unexpected.

Unable to resist, Jake pulled his mouth off and looked under the man's crotch. A bent metal bar pierced his perineum.

Jake had never seen such a thing, though he'd heard of it. It turned him on. He stroked the man's cock with his hand and buried his face behind his balls, licking his taint and fiddling with the piercing with his tongue. The older man groaned.

Jake felt himself grow hard. He had a thing for older men and pleasuring this guy was a fantasy come true. He continued licking and probing with his tongue, stroking with his hand, until the moans continued non-stop. Although, the man's dick still wasn't hard. He returned his laving to the cock in his hands. It needed vigorous attention.

He glanced up and saw both men pinching each other's nipples. The portly man's shirt was bunched under his armpits. They leaned in and kissed each other, their tongues wrapping around each other.

Jake didn't understand the attraction, but didn't concern himself with it. He sucked the man's cock, stretching it out with every repetition. Perhaps it was one of those dicks that didn't get hard.

He could make the best of it. Since it wasn't hard, Jake stuffed it all into his mouth. It was thick and his jaw barely stretched to accommodate, but he managed to get the entire thing inside him. He ran his tongue over what he could, then slowly pulled his head away, stretching the cock out again. Jake massaged the man's testicles with his fingers.

The man let out a deep moan that resonated through his body. The firm and gentle hand from before rested on Jake's head again. The grip tensed momentarily and the man's cum spilled into Jake's mouth, hot and salty.

Jake swallowed it and, like with the other man, slowly removed himself from the cock and gently licked it clean. He looked up. The older man was flushed and stared down at Jake, eyes hazy. The portly man was nibbling on the older man's neck.

"Thanks," the man said, breathless.

Jake winked. "I hope you guy's don't mind, but I have to get those muffins in the oven. Can I kick you out of the kitchen?"

"Of course," the man said. He pulled up his pajamas and followed the bear out of the room, fondling his ass as they went.

As the door closed, Jake heard one man ask the other, "Are you at this hostel much longer?"

Jake blinked several times to clear the unbidden imagery from his mind. There were some things that were perhaps best left behind closed doors.

He pulled himself to his feet and slapped his knees several times to clear the dust from them, then washed his hands and returned to his baking. As he watched the batter flow between the beaters, he fought back and emptiness that opened in his heart and threatened to overcome it. The feeling had gotten stronger the longer he was away from Canada.

Maybe sucking off Grant will be the one that works.

He shook his head and pulled a set of muffin trays out of the lower cupboard.

Chapter Three

J AKE RAN HIS HAND THROUGH HIS towel-dried hair and walked through the dining area to the kitchen. The two men from last night sat at the table together, very closely. He tried not to stare as the older man's hand slid down the other man's back toward his ass.

He shook his head and pushed through the door to the kitchen. Thankfully, the horde of Russians had left first thing in the morning, so not only was it quieter, but there also wasn't a pile of dishes in the sink.

Jake pulled his bread out of the fridge and dropped the last two slices in the toaster. He bit back a curse and tossed the bag—he'd have to go across the bridge today for more. After his toast popped up, he dug out his jar of Nutella and slathered it on thick. Given what the Russians did yesterday, he'd have to buy more Nutella too.

"Afternoon. Or, I guess it's morning for you."

Jake smiled and turned around. He hadn't heard Grant enter. "Good morning to you too." Jake eyed the man up and down. Unfortunately, he'd swapped yesterday's kilt out for a pair of jeans and a T-shirt, though they fit him almost as well as the kilt did. "How was your first night?"

"Glorious—it's so quiet here. Total opposite of Edinburgh." Grant dug sandwich ingredients out of the fridge.

"Cool...cool...Anyway, like I said yesterday, if you need anything after midnight, I'm your guy."

There was an odd twitch to Grant's eyes. "Yeah, I remember. I'll keep that in mind, mate."

Jake leaned against the counter and munched on his toast as he watched Grant assemble his meal. The man was a mystery; Jake couldn't figure him out. All he knew was he made something stir deep inside. Jake wanted him. Almost as much as...

"Tell me about yourself," Jake finally said. "You live in Edinburgh and work in IT. But what else? What are your hobbies? Do you have a girlfriend...or boyfriend?" He watched the Scot's face intently when he asked about love interests. Grant didn't flinch at the suggestion of a boyfriend, so that told Jake the man was probably gay or bi...and might be open to a midnight blowjob.

"Not much to say, really. I like to read and play video

games." His eyes locked with Jake's for the briefest moment. "And I'm currently single."

Definitely gay…or bi.

Since he didn't seem to be opening up, Jake switched topics. "What brought you to Kyleakin—the ass-end of nowhere?"

Grant put his knife and mustard jar down on the counter and stared at Jake uncomfortably.

Jake swallowed his toast. "What?"

Grant narrowed his eyes. "I'm trying to figure out if you were joking or you don't actually know the beauty of Skye."

He felt a blush warm his cheeks and he looked away. "I'm more of a city boy. I grew up in Canada's version of the ass-end of nowhere. I've had enough of that."

It took a long moment for Grant's glare to dissipate. He crossed his arms and leaned against the counter. "So have you never explored Skye beyond Kyleakin?"

"I took the bus up to Portree for a look around. Didn't see much."

"But what about the scenery on the way?"

Jake looked away again. "I kind of slept the whole way there and back."

"Oh my God," Grant muttered and resumed his sandwich making. "Did you say you have a day off this week? We need to go for a drive."

"I, uh, have Friday and Saturday off."

"Good." Grant smiled. "It's a date."

A queasy flutter rippled through Jake's gut. He wanted to suck dick, not find a boyfriend. *It's a figure of speech. Calm down.*

Jake fought past his unease to force a smile. "Sounds like a plan." He quickly washed his plate and knife. "Now, if you'll excuse me, I've got to go across the bridge to get some bread. Do you need anything?"

Grant smiled. "No, but thanks."

Hoping that Grant didn't pick up on too much of his discomfort, Jake hiked back up to his room to get his shoes. He laced them up and walked back down, greeting Audra along the way. Like always, she sat behind the desk watching a video of some sort. A warm afternoon greeted him when he stepped out the door. Kyleakin was a tiny village, no bigger than his hometown of Grayson, though considerably more picturesque. As beautiful as it was, it was still way too small for him. He wanted the hustle and bustle, the life and hurry of a busy city.

The hostel was located on one of two parallel streets. Jake took a crossroad over to Kyleside, which put the village on one side of him and the very blue Loch Alsh on his other side. The sun was bright and warm as he wandered to the long, gray bridge that connected the Isle of Skye to the mainland and the village of Kyle of Localsh. It was a trek to get to the other side, but it allowed him to escape from everything and just focus on the sounds of gulls and waves.

Though Kyle of Localsh wasn't all that much larger than Kyleakin, it at least had a fully stocked grocery store. After purchasing bread, Nutella, and a few other items and making the forty-five minute walk back to the hostel, Jake carefully labeled his food and put them in the fridge and cupboard.

The hostel was quiet at this time of day. Soon, people would return from their hikes and day trips to make themselves dinner and relax in the common room for the evening. Other than hanging out at one of the pubs, there wasn't much to do in Kyleakin after dinner. Sporadically about the hostel were a handful of people engaged in quiet activities; reading, cards, video calls with family back home. Jake quickly ran up to his room and grabbed his notebook and pen, then slipped silently out the front door.

He hiked to the end of the village's main road and merged onto a worn footpath through the bushes and grass. The scramble up the hill was a little rough, but he knew the steadiest path. Ahead and above him were the ruins of Dunakin Castle, a crumbling mass of brown and gray stone.

Jake wound his way around the castle ruin to his favorite spot. He sat down on the soft grass, resting his back against the smooth façade of the remains of Dunakin Castle. His resting spot was enough inside the castle ruins that he felt ensconced in some place older than time and full of wonder, yet not so far in that the deteriorating structure was any danger to him. The contradictory appeal didn't escape him—he was a big city boy at heart, but loved the quiet country ruin.

In front of him, down the steep slope, sprawled Loch Alsh, a large body of deep blue water, with wave tops sparkling in the late afternoon sun. Across the expanse lay Kyle of Localsh, its bright white buildings gleaming. Jake opened his notebook and flipped to a blank page.

He lay back against the stone wall and watched the water. Boats glided across its surface or anchored just off shore. This was a place he found inspiring, one worthy of bringing inspiration to his poetry writing.

He put his pen to the paper and...did nothing. Just like yesterday. Just like every day.

He flipped through the mostly-clean pages until he found the letter he'd attempted to write the day before. No matter how long Jake stared at it, the right words just didn't want to form. How could he tell Peter what he wanted to say? There was so much to it...and so much more he couldn't admit. He flipped back to the blank page. The letter was yesterday. Poetry was today.

Jake closed his eyes; nothing came. Poetic inspiration couldn't be forced, but he couldn't sit here three or four times a week waiting for that ever-elusive muse to arrive. The notebook had been new when he arrived in Scotland, filled with fresh, virgin pages and bound in leather. A gift from Peter. Almost a year later and they were still almost all unmarked. Maybe it was the notebook—a gift like this from a man like that…it almost felt blasphemous to write anything less than perfect on its crisp pages.

Something wasn't working in his life. Something was missing. He knew what it was. Rather, he knew *who* it was.

He heard the crunch of a footstep on gravel from around the corner. Jake closed his notebook and stared out at the water. He didn't want to be disturbed and learned from experience that an open notebook invited questions from people he didn't want to talk to.

"Oh, hello."

Jake looked up. Grant stood near with a small backpack slung over his shoulder and a sheen of sweat across his forehead. His T-shirt, which had been deliciously tight just a couple hours ago, now clung even closer to his skin, body moisture holding it in place.

"Hey, Grant. Out for a hike?"

As much as Jake wanted to know what the Scot was packing in his jeans, he still didn't really want to talk to him here. This was his place of solitude, his place to get away from everything, all the pressures and limitations of life and just…just be.

"Yeah." Grant pulled a water bottle out of his pack and took a long swig. His Adam's apple bobbed prominently with each swallow. "I started from the hostel and went west for a good half hour or so before doubling back and now going as far east as possible. When I saw this ruin ahead of me, I couldn't pass up the opportunity."

Jake smiled and looked at the water again. "It's a special place."

"That it is." Grant dropped his backpack to the ground and dug out his camera. This vantage point offered an amazing view of the local surroundings, so Jake wasn't surprised to hear Grant's camera chirp with every shot he took.

"If you really want something special, you need to come back at sundown. It's a bit risky, but if you carefully crawl down this slope," Jake pointed down toward the water, "and take a picture of the castle, you can get the sunset behind the ruins. If you get your timing right and the weather is perfect, you can get a deep pink sky outlining the silhouette of the castle. Of course, the dangerous part is trying to find your way back in the dark—the path isn't quite so level."

Grant eyed the slope down toward the water and then the castle. "Wow. That sounds romantic."

That same stomach burbling of discomfort returned. "Yeah, I guess." He wished the man would shut up about romance and dates.

Grant pulled out his phone and glanced at the time. "I was going to head back and make something to eat. You want to join me? I make a mean chicken pesto."

Jake shook his head. "No, I think I'm going to hang out here for a while."

Grant shrugged and then sat next to Jake. Their shoulders brushed and heat grew between them. "Are you writing something?" he asked, nodding toward Jake's notebook.

"Not really. Well, I'm trying. It's my poetry book. I've really gotten out of it this past year and I'm trying to dive back in."

"Oh? Is there something you're willing to share? Or is it private?"

"It's private. Sorry."

"No worries." Grant smiled contentedly and leaned against the wall.

"It's kind of, well, empty. It just hasn't been coming to me these past several months." Jake didn't know why he felt the urge to elaborate.

"I'm sure you'll get back into it soon." Grant shifted into a more comfortable position, pushing his body more firmly against Jake's.

Jake wiggled, inching away. He kept waiting for Grant to get up and leave, but he didn't seem to take the hint.

After several minutes of what was for Jake a very uncomfortable silence, Grant finally stood and picked up his backpack. "Well, I'll head back then. I'll see you later?"

"For sure," Jake said. As Grant walked away, he decided to fish once again. "And remember—anything you need after midnight, I'm your guy."

Grant smiled over his shoulder. "I'll remember that."

With solitude returned to him, Jake closed his eyes and absorbed the sounds of nature around him. He didn't open his notebook again. His letter to Peter had waited ten months; it could wait a little longer.

When the sun began to set, and it looked like this wasn't going to be a spectacular sunset, he carefully picked his way down the footpath to the street. He wandered down past the pubs, both well lit and half-full, and veered toward the fish and chips stand, arriving minutes before it closed.

He ordered a combo and took it down to the beach. He kicked off his shoes and sat down in the sand in just the perfect spot—far enough back to keep his ass dry and forward enough for the waves to lap at his toes. Jake ate the fish and chips, licking the grease off his fingers.

Night had fallen and the beach was illuminated by the moon and stars. The town behind him was almost completely dark. A few lonely streetlights cast feeble pools of resistance against the oncoming black.

Jake sighed. It was about time to head in and get ready for his shift. Instead, he fell back against the sand and stared up at the stars.

Chapter Four

JAKE RIPPED OPEN A NEW BOX OF BISCUIT mix and dumped half of it in the large metal bowl. He pulled out the measuring cup and filled it with water, dumping it in too. Perhaps it would be wiser to hold off on digging his hands in the dough, given the past two nights. Curious, he silently crept toward the kitchen door and listened. There was no noise—not a footstep nor a creak on the stairs.

Disappointed at another night without getting to hold and taste Grant's cock, Jake squished his fingers in the dough and worked it to the proper consistency. He scooped out little balls and dropped them on the baking sheet and put them in the oven. A short while later, a couple dozen biscuits cooled on the counter.

Jake grimaced. His next task was to clean the bathrooms. His most hated task. Switching off the kitchen lights, he quietly made his way to the supply cupboard, grabbed the cleaning caddy and started with the main floor washrooms. They were unisex facilities, which meant no urinals to contend with, just three stalls and three sinks. The upstairs washrooms were more of a chore with their accompanying shower stalls, so those were always last on his list.

As he crouched in front of one of the toilets to scrub, the bathroom door opened. It wasn't unusual for one of the guests near the stairs to come to this washroom rather than go down the hall to the one on their floor.

"You said you'd be in the kitchen."

Jake's heart pounded against his ribs and his cock stirred in his pants.

He peeled off his rubber gloves and dropped them in the caddy, coming out of the stall to find Grant standing in a rather tight pair of boxer briefs, and nothing else. His chest, abs, arms, and legs were tightly honed from what looked like a life of sport and physical activity and covered in a smattering of fur. The dick in his underwear was hard, thick, and pointed sideways, the tight fabric revealing every bump and ridge.

Jake did his best to grin seductively. "I'm glad you made the effort to find me."

Although it was approaching a quarter to three in the morning, their chance of discovery in the washroom was slightly higher than in the kitchen, so Jake walked past Grant to lock the door.

"I think you know why I'm here," Grant said, voice deep and low.

"You want me to play your bagpipes."

Grant snickered. "That was bad, you know. Really bad."

Jake winked. "I don't know if I have to work on seducing you so much if you're already here."

"Point taken."

Jake walked toward Grant, hand outstretched to grasp the man's cock. He ran his fingers along the length of Grant's shaft, feeling the ridges and the bulb of his head. A small dot of precum wet the gray fabric.

Grant raised his hand to Jake's chest and felt his nipples through his T-shirt. On instinct, Jake gently grabbed the man's hand and brought it down.

"This is about you, not me," Jake said, covering for the sudden awkwardness of having brushed Grant away.

As Jake lowered himself to the floor, Grant put a hand on either side of Jake's face and pulled him back up, bringing him close. Jake could tell what he wanted, but held back. His heart thumped, but not with lust. The cold rush of anxiety coursed through him.

"Kiss me," Grant whispered.

The Scot leaned in, eyes closed, lips puckered. Jake turned his head and the kiss landed on his ear. He hoped that would satisfy him, and bent his knees to lower himself again, but Grant held on tight.

He looked up at the Scot. His eyes were open and he examined Jake with questioning. "Kiss me."

Jake looked away. "I just want to suck your big cock."

Grant's eyelids lowered a little. "Why won't you kiss me?"

Jake stepped back out of Grant's hold. The man's hands fell down to his side. "I don't kiss," Jake said, looking at the floor. He tamped down pent-up emotions that threatened to burst free. "It's too intimate."

When Grant didn't respond, Jake glanced back up at him. His expression was bewildered. "Too intimate?" he finally said. "You're about to put your mouth on my cock and suck the cum out of me. How is a kiss too intimate?"

Jake looked at the walls, the mirrors, the sinks, anywhere but in Grant's eyes. He rubbed his right elbow absently. "It just is."

"I don't...I don't know what to say. I don't bloody understand this. How is a kiss more intimate than a blowjob?" Grant's expression had turned from confusion to anger, and his voice grew louder.

"Just forget it, okay?" Jake unlocked the door behind him. He looked at the floor again. "This obviously isn't going to happen."

"You're right it's not going to happen." He strode past Jake and out of the bathroom. Before the door fully closed, Grant muttered, "Wanker."

When the door clicked and silence returned, Jake moved woodenly to the stall and pulled on the rubber gloves. He knelt before the toilet and resumed scrubbing.

Moisture collected in his eyes and threatened to become tears. Jake sniffled and wiped his arm against his nose. The cold anxiety had dissipated with the threat of a kiss now gone, but the heat of anger replaced it.

Fucking Grant. High and mighty asshole.

The more he scrubbed the more his thoughts simmered, and the more those thoughts grew angrier. Grant had no right to judge him. Everyone was different—so what if he didn't kiss. You don't need kissing to get into the receiving end of a fucking blowjob.

Grant needs to get his head out of his fucking ass.

A part of him, deep inside somewhere, yearned for attention…a long-ago touch, a forgotten embrace, an ignored attraction…

Before those painful memories could resurface, he shoved them back down and focused on his ire.

Fucking Scotsman. Asshole.

Jake had taken a peek at the guest registry after he'd first spotted Grant—he was here until Sunday morning, which meant he had almost a whole week ahead of him having to share his living space with that arrogant prick.

Grant can take his fucking kisses and kiss his own fucking ass.

Chapter Five

Monday, 11:50 AM

FRESHLY SHOWERED WITH EVERY every square inch clean, Jake descended from the staff dorm in the attic. He wore his casual clothes—not as put-together as his outfit usually was, but they were an easy fit and slipped off quickly.

As expected, Audra was working the front desk. She was a local from Oban or somewhere, Jake could never remember. She was rail-thin with a head full of curly brown hair. The most important fact, though, was that she had a car.

Jake put on his best smile as he approached the desk. Audra was watching videos on the company laptop, again, while munching on a deep-fried Mars bar. Even from several feet away, he saw the glistening fingerprints on the keys—solving the mystery of who the idiot was who kept making the keyboard slick.

"Morning, Audra," Jake said, trying not to glare at the oily prints.

She looked at him strangely, then at the clock on the wall. "Wow...it *is* morning. What are you up so early for?"

"Oh, nothing." Jake leaned forward to see what was playing on the laptop. He arched an eyebrow.

"It's adorable," Audra said. "There're these crows somewhere in Russia that are using snowy windscreens as toboggan runs—look! He's rolling down!" She laughed loudly and clapped her hands. Crumbs from her "food" sprinkled across the desk.

"Yeah," Jake said, "cute."

"Aww, did someone get up on the wrong side of the bed?"

"No, I—"

"Here, have some Mars bar!" She shoved the greasy, paper-wrapped item in his face.

He restrained himself considerably and only gently nudged her hand back. "No, thanks. You know what I think about them."

She rolled her eyes. "You really don't know what you're missing."

"Anyway," he said, stressing the word. "I'm up early for a reason. I was kind of hoping to maybe borrow your car for the day. Pretty please?"

"Where you going?" She bit off another mouthful of candy bar and clicked to a new video, leaving another glistening smear on the trackpad.

"Inverness. I need some big city excitement for the day."

Audra scoffed. "*Big city.* Inverness is hardly a big city."

Jake struggled to keep his irritation under wraps. "Biggest one in the area. So can I borrow your car?"

She stared hard at him. "Last time you brought it back with an empty tank—you have to top up the petrol before you return it."

He put on his most winning smile. "Of course. Sorry about last time, I'll do better today."

She looked at him hard. "Okay, you can take it. But…you have to do something for me."

"Anything. Just name it."

"Have a bite of my Mars bar. You're too thin." She held the bar up to his face, greasy paper almost translucent.

Jake closed his eyes, opened his mouth, and took a bite. It was actually better than he'd expected.

Almost two hours later, Jake regretted taking that mouthful of chocolate. He'd always been sensitive to oily foods and his stomach growled to remind him of that fact yet again. Stifling his discomfort, he maneuvered the car into the city of Inverness and quickly found a parking spot. After stopping in a bakery to get a small sandwich to settle his stomach, Jake walked over to his primary destination, the whole reason he borrowed Audra's car.

The Brawny Scot.

The building was unmarked. Jake had only found the bathhouse—or sauna, as he learned the Scots called it—

previously via the internet. He went in the entry to a locked hallway; a small window opened next to the door and eyes peered out at him, giving him a quick glance over. A soft buzzer sounded and Jake pushed his way through.

The space beyond the main desk was dark with harsh pools of light. Jake knew the routine; he handed over his ID, not required of all guests, just those that appeared younger like him.

"Room or locker?" The man behind the desk was unshaven and had a missing tooth that brought a whistle to his words. Long, stringy hair hung about his shoulders. A porn video on mute played on the TV behind him.

"Locker."

"Six quid."

Jake pulled the dirty coins out of his pocket and lay them on the counter. The man grabbed them and handed Jake a white towel and a key attached to an elastic armband.

Jake walked around the corner toward the lockers, his eyes adjusting to the progressively dim lighting. A couple guys wandered the halls, wearing only their towels. They eyed Jake hungrily.

The locker area was around a final bend in the corridor. Jake quickly stripped naked, stuffed his clothes inside his locker, tied the towel low around his waist, and strung the key on his left bicep.

It had been too long since his last visit to the sauna. There wasn't anything like this back home in rural

Saskatchewan. So, while The Brawny Scot could be a bit of a dive compared to some of the saunas and bathhouses he'd seen on the internet, it was *his* sauna. It was his place to get down and dirty, something he needed when something stirred up his past and old emotions. A good hedonistic time would help bury those things again.

Walking through the gloomy and twisting corridors, he passed the occasional older man similarly clad in nothing but a towel. Given the time of day, the place was likely filled with mostly retired men, probably on a midday break from the wife. Though that meant the cock was slightly older and more wrinkled than Jake preferred, he was still going to make the best of it.

First, though, he needed to relax and release the stress and tension that Grant brought him. In one dark corner were shadowy outlines of two men—one standing and the other kneeling before him. The rhythmic sounds of sucking followed Jake around the final corridor to the hot tub. He stripped off his towel, semi-hard dick bouncing with the movement, and stepped into the half-full tub.

He met the eyes of each of the three other men in turn, assessing them. The first was older, perhaps sixty, a little portly and with a forest of white hair across his chest. His eyes twinkled lecherously at Jake. The second man was much younger, maybe late thirties or early forties, with a head of thick, black hair and a smooth, shaved chest. The third man's age was in-between the other two and his pale blond hair seemed almost white in the gloomy light.

In the water, the jets and currents brushed against Jake's cock, making it harder. The thought of being in the tub with three naked men, despite them not being Adonis-like, solidified his dick.

"Hi," Jake said, smiling as he looked at each man again.

The two younger men had probably come together, as they ignored Jake and stared only at each other. Their hands were moving vigorously underneath the water, despite a large sign on the wall that declared "No sex and no wanking in the hot tub."

"We don't see many lads like you," the furry-chested man said.

Jake smiled. "Come here often, I assume?"

Despite lecherous eyes, the man's face was kind and gentle. "I do. I like to relax and unwind and this place helps."

"Yeah, I've been here a couple times before. It's a nice place."

"You're not from around here, are you?" The man tilted his head a few degrees and squinted as he thought. "Your accent…Canadian?"

"Very impressive. How did you know?"

"Oh, practice, I guess. I used to travel a lot for work and met a lot of different people." The man shuffled in his seat, coming a couple feet closer to Jake. "So what brings you to Scotland?"

"Just a year of working abroad to escape the monotony of home." Jake glanced at the two younger men again. Their movements were getting more vigorous and enthusiastic. The blond whispered something in the other's ear and they soon climbed out of the hot tub, grabbed their towels, and disappeared down a dark corridor. He looked back at the older man, who inched closer to him.

Before the older man could lay a hand on Jake's leg, for that was surely coming, he stood up. "I think I'm going to check out the sauna and stuff. Was nice meeting you." Jake offered the man a smile and climbed out, grabbing his towel and drying himself off before wrapping it back around his waist.

He wasn't exactly opposed to fooling around with that man, but he wanted to see what the rest of the place had to offer before giving the guy a tug or blow. Someone in a chat room once told him that saunas and bath houses get busy after midnight, and that's when the hot young men come out. Daytimes, like right now, were mostly the retired men, which was exactly the same as his last daytime visit. So, in all likelihood, he'd be hooking up with men more than twice his age…which wasn't always a bad thing.

The corridor was dark and had several corners and hideaways. Eventually, Jake saw a dim light ahead and emerged into a semi-lit area with two showerheads and two doors. He hung his towel on the hook and took a quick rinse, completely out in the open, before grabbing his towel again and stepping through the door into the dry sauna. It was as dim as everywhere else, with little more than the faint shapes of other men in the room.

He unwrapped himself again, placing the towel down below him. Jake sat, keeping his legs closed, being careful not to send an invitation. As his eyes adjusted to the light, he began to make out the other bodies. Most seemed to be in their late thirties or early forties, with decent figures. It didn't seem to be quite the seniors' outing he'd expected. No one made eye contact, though. One person slowly stroked his dick in the corner.

After sitting there for several minutes, Jake stood and wrapped the towel around his waist again. He exited and then went in the second door, entering the wet sauna. There was no one in there, so he set out his towel again and sat down. Leaning back, Jake closed his eyes as the steam surrounded him.

The click of the door announced an arrival. Jake made sure his legs were in the closed position to ward off unwanted advances. In his mind, he imagined all the cocks he'd seen in the sauna lined up for his mouth. And in his lap, his dick thickened.

The newcomer chuckled. "We meet again."

Jake opened one eye. The furry-chested man from the hot tub sat across from him. He, too, had laid the towel out below him and was as naked as Jake. His legs were spread wide open.

He took the opportunity to check out the older man. Jake's gaze wandered up and down the man, lingering long as he took in the sight of the thick and cleanly-shaven cock between the man's legs. His mouth watered.

The man must have noticed the ogling, as his hand dropped into his lap and fondled his monstrous dick, stirring it to life. "So what are you here for today?"

Jake couldn't help from grinning. "I'm here for cock. A lot of it."

"Oh, yeah?" The man's dick had stiffened and elongated.

"Yeah, but not here." Jake licked his lips. "I'm going to set myself up in the glory hole booth in a few minutes."

The man's eyebrows danced up and down a couple times. "A lad with a plan. Sexy."

Jake eyed the door. "Can you do me a favor?"

"Of course." The man fiddled with one of his nipples, buried under the tangled mass of hair. "What do you need?"

"I want to get as much as I can. If you could go in the other sauna and strike up a short conversation with somebody—tell him that you saw the hot, young guy go in the glory booths or something—and say it loud enough that everyone can hear you."

"You're dirty," the man said with a smirk. His hand slid up and down his dick, moist with sweat and glistening with precum.

"And I want that," Jake said, nodding at the man's crotch, "to be my last one. End it with the biggest of all."

The man eyed Jake. "On one condition. After you suck me, I want to suck you."

Jake looked down at his lap, at the still thickening dick sprawled over his leg. "I don't normally let anyone suck me off, but if you do this for me, then I'll make an exception."

The man winked. "Deal." He stood and picked up his towel. He didn't bother wrapping it around his waist before exiting and crossing to the dry sauna.

Jake's heart quickened as he stood up and covered himself with the towel. He'd been dreaming of this all day. All night, really, ever since Grant demanded that fucking kiss. It was his only escape.

He exited the wet sauna and wandered through a second dark, winding corridor. This one was lined with doors to private rooms. Some were open with naked men lounging on the beds. At the end of the hall was a small lounge area with a leather couch, a muted TV with porn, and a closet-like cubicle with a hole cut in the wall.

Jake made sure the booth was unoccupied, then entered the cramped area. There was a plastic stool and nothing else. It was lit with a weak, red, bare light bulb hanging above his head. His foot landed in something slick, but he tried not to think too much of it. Hanging the towel on the doorknob, Jake sat bare-assed on the stool, dangling his fingertips out of the glory hole to signal his desire to service.

Not more than a few minutes later, Jake noticed movement through the hole and quickly angled his head to get a better look. True to his word, the older man had four others with him. Before he could make eye contact with any of them, Jake backed away from the hole. He didn't want them to see his face or for him to see theirs; this was to be as anonymous as possible. *The exact opposite of Grant and his fucking intimacy.*

Seconds later, the first man thrust his dick through the glory hole. Jake wrapped his fingers around it. It was a standard cock—not too big, not too small, not too thick. As he pressed his lips to it and took it into his mouth, his own dick finally rose to full attention, hardening with each heartbeat. It was hot and tasted of sweat, probably right from the sauna.

He bounced his head back and forth rhythmically, working up a good sucking routine. With one hand wrapped tightly around the base of the man's cock, Jake fondled the tight sack that hugged close to the base and just barely protruded through the hole.

Jake sucked the air out of his mouth, creating a tight vacuum. Slowing his pace, he slid his mouth down as far as he could, lips just barely touching the man's groin. Jake slid his mouth all the way off and then all the way back on to the hilt again.

He felt a small quiver run through the man's body and his already-tight balls tightened some more. Jake resumed his rapid back-and-forth, working up a fervor to drive the man over his edge. With a deep and loud groan, hot cum spurted into his mouth. Jake immediately pulled the cock out of his mouth, catching all of the cum on his cheeks, chin, and chest.

On any other day, he'd swallow it, but Jake felt particularly dirty today. Long strands hung from his chin, dribbling down to land on his nipples. The taste left on his tongue was a little bitter, but still delicious. The man's cock slowly deflated.

The man backed away and was replaced by another. This cock was thick, but not hard, and had a Prince Albert pierced through the slit. Glistening precum dripped from the man like a faucet.

Jake brushed his lips across the man's slit, gathering all the clear precum on his lips. He tasted it with his tongue, then took the dick slowly into his mouth. He'd never sucked a PA before; the metal slid over his tongue and added an interesting sensation.

No matter how hard he sucked, the guy's cock wouldn't get hard. He must have just been one of those people that never got fully solid, like the old man the other night. It didn't discourage Jake. He sucked fast and furious. With a softer dick, Jake was able to take the entire thing in his mouth if he opened wide.

He stopped his bobbing when he had the entire cock in his mouth. Jake ran his tongue over what he could, then again sucked out all of the air from his mouth, creating a tighter seal. A moan sounded through the thin wall; this was good for him.

Jake worked up the speed and rhythm he had with the first guy. It wasn't long before this cock, too, spilled precious cum into his mouth. Again, he quickly pulled it out, allowing a heavy load to cover his face and chest, adding it to the mess from the first guy. Globs rolled down over this abs. This second man's cum tasted a bit saltier, but still delicious. Jake never could get enough of the stuff.

The second cock disappeared and was immediately replaced by the third. This was a short and stubby one, not difficult at all to swallow in its entirety. With this one, Jake swirled his tongue all around the cock and over the head and past the slit. The muscles in his tongue soon tired, but he continued with his laving. This man was a quick comer. Another load hit his tongue and Jake pulled back to let it coat him. Cum covered his chest and dripped down his torso, the essence of three men mingling together.

The fourth man had a long and thin dick, and was far more vocal than the others. Whereas the first three men had mostly been silent, this one moaned and groaned loudly, as if wanting the entire sauna to know that he was getting blown. Jake sucked him fast and hard, not because he enjoyed the man's obvious pleasure, but because he wanted him to shut up. Thankfully, this man was almost as quick a comer as the third guy. Moments later, with a roar of climax, a fourth load of cum coated Jake's chin and chest.

After that cock pulled back from the glory hole, the portly older man's immense meat slid through. Jake grinned wickedly, cum dripping from his chin and landing on his legs. He was going to tease this man a little, work him up to an explosive finish.

Jake put his mouth close to the cock without touching it and exhaled hot breath over the length of it. The man's dick twitched and bounced. Jake shuffled to the other side and repeated the breathing, earning more twitches in response. He then stuck out his tongue and ran just the tip of it up and down the length and around the ridge of the head. With each repetition, he pressed harder with his tongue and used more of its surface, until he was forcefully dragging his entire tongue up and down the man's length and girth.

Jake then took the man's cock in his mouth, moving slowly, inch by inch toward its base. The cum still coating his lips acted as lube, slicking the man's dick. He could only get about halfway before his mouth was filled beyond capacity. With a tight grip, he wrapped his hand around the other half. He stroked and bobbed his head in rhythm.

He hooked a finger through the hole and pulled the man's low-hanging balls through. They rested against the dividing wall. Jake wrapped his hand around them, giving them the occasional sharp tug. Jake took the man as deep as he could again, gagging as the head of the cock hit the back of his throat. Pulling it almost all the way out, he tightened his lips in a circle and ran them vigorously back and forth over the ridge of the man's head. The cock jolted suddenly as the man's knees wobbled at the intense pleasure, knocking against the barrier between them. Jake alternated between taking it deep a few times and rubbing the head with his lips.

As the ache set in his jaw, the man's balls tightened and before Jake could react, a large shot filled his mouth. He pulled his lips off the cock and watched in amazement as several more very large shots covered his face and chest, producing far more than the other four guys. As the spurts came to an end and long dribbles hung from the tip of his cock, Jake carefully licked him clean, getting the last of his cum. It was salty and sweet, heavenly, drowning out the taste of the other four men.

When the cock was finally soft and glisteningly clean, the man pulled it back.

Jake stood up, shook out his knees, and grabbed the towel, not bothering to tie it around his waist. He had to hold up his end of the bargain. Exiting the booth, the only man remaining was the portly older man with the furry chest. *Good.* He had wanted it as anonymous as possible; he'd never know who the other four cocks belonged to.

The man's eyes widened as his gaze moved up and down Jake's cum-covered face and torso, then narrowed hungrily as his sight settled on Jake's rock hard cock. Jake smiled a sticky grin.

Without words, the man pointed at the small leather couch at the other end of the small open area. Jake put the towel down and laid on it as the man got down on his knees and immediately took Jake in his mouth.

Jake moaned and ran his hands across his cum-covered chest. He rubbed the sticky fluid all over his chest, rubbing it in, then ran his hands up his neck and into his mouth, tasting all of the men. Pleasure rippled from his cock as the man sucked with practiced ease and expertise.

The only thing that would make this moment better is if it were Grant the one doing this to him.

Jake's eyes flared open. *What the fuck?*

Why had his mind gone there? Grant was nothing but a pain in the ass, and not the good kind.

"Mmm…you're enjoying this."

Jake looked down at the grinning man. He held Jake's very rigid and dripping cock in his hand.

Jake was at a loss for words. Deep inside, he knew it wasn't the blowjob making him leak like crazy. And though this man was good, it wasn't him making Jake this hard. He nodded, trying to appear too into the act to speak.

The man returned his attention to Jake's dick, saving him from having to respond further. He wasn't sure if he'd be able to put together words right now.

What the fuck...? What the fuck...? His thoughts quieted as he submerged into the rush of the blowjob.

Jake closed his eyes and tried to think of nothing but the hot mouth on his dick. But he soon imagined Grant deep throating him. He smiled as the heat filled him. This was a good thought, no matter how much Grant irritated him.

Confusion rippled through Jake's mind as the image of Grant sucking him wavered and began to change, morphing into another familiar face. Before the new face revealed itself, electricity surged through Jake as his long-denied orgasm overwhelmed him. His hips bucked wildly against the couch, shoving his dick deeper into the man's mouth. Loud, wordless grunts came from his mouth and he screwed his eyes shut as all that uncontainable energy came to a head and shot out of him.

He gasped and shuddered as he shot several times into the man's mouth. The man swallowed as Jake filled him, the movements of the tongue sending more pleasure through Jake's cock. As the well of energy left him, every muscle went loose in Jake's body as he relaxed fully and completely on the couch. Jake took several long and deep breaths to regain the strength and composure to move and speak.

"Th-thank you," Jake said. When there was no reply, he opened his eyes. The foyer was empty; the TV lit the space in dim flesh tones.

That orgasm had been amazing. That guy had been phenomenal. This was all he had hoped to get today, and more. But if this was what he had wanted so badly, then why did his chest feel so empty right now? This place was supposed to bury unwanted emotions…but today it just set them loose.

He shook his head and stood up, pausing to let his knees regain stability. He looked down at his chest in the weak light. It glistened and sparkled. Part of him was turned on by what he'd just done, but a small part of him was a bit repulsed and just wanted to have a hot shower. He grabbed his towel and wandered back to the locker area, running his tongue over his fuzzy teeth.

The lockers were mercifully empty. For once, Jake felt he'd had his daily fill of cocks and cum. There was a showerhead at the end of the row of lockers, as out in the open as the other shower had been. He turned it to as hot as he could handle and stood under the stream.

Jake rubbed his hand across his chest, loosening some partially-dried cum. He watched it run down the length of his body and through the grated drain between his feet. As the visual evidence of what he'd done washed away, he was left with only his thoughts and feelings.

He smirked, thinking of Grant's reaction if he could have seen what Jake had just done. But what did those images during the blowjob mean? He'd envisioned Grant sucking him off…then the image of him had wavered…he was pretty sure it was turning into Peter…

His thoughts were interrupted as a man came around the corner and found the locker he'd been assigned. The man was tall and muscular, a DILF if Jake had ever seen one. Between Jake's legs, his spent cock experienced the first twitchings of stirring back to life.

The man was watching Jake out of the corner of his eye as he undressed. Jake wasn't up for another round—he had to get back to the hostel and shower properly with soap and everything before starting work. He shut off the water and found his locker, quickly throwing it open and avoiding all eye contact with the other man.

Thankfully, by the time he'd pulled on his underwear, the man had retreated around the corner and into the darkness. Jake quickly threw on the rest of his clothes and handed in his towel and key.

"Have a good time?" the man at the desk asked. The man's missing teeth continued to bring a whistle to his words.

Jake faked a satisfied face and gave the man a wink. "You bet. Had a fantasy fulfilled."

The man laughed with a gentle wheeze. His long white hair bounced over his shoulders. "A few guys have been walking around with smiles. Were you the twink in the booth?"

Jake laughed. "Yeah, that's me."

"You made a few men very happy today." As the man took Jake's key from him, he handed him a card. "Take this. It's a free admission for next time. We need more young studs like you here."

"Thanks." Jake tucked the card in his back pocket, unsure if he wanted to return if this place had lost its effectiveness on him. "I'll see you again, then."

The man winked at Jake and returned to his computer, pressing play on the porn video he'd been in the midst of watching.

After the long drive back to Kyleakin, with a stop for petrol in Kyle of Localsh just before the bridge, Jake returned the keys to Audra. Marching up the steps to the staff dorm in the attic, he passed Grant on the stairs. The Scot was wearing his kilt again, with his hairy, muscular legs out in full glory. If Jake wasn't so pissed at the man, his dick probably would've gotten rock hard at the sight.

"Where were you all day?" Grant asked. His eyes searched Jake's face and then locked on a spot on his neck. Had Jake missed a spot of cum?

"Out. If you'll excuse me, I need to shower—my shift starts in an hour." He had set out to do a metaphorical "eff you" to Grant and his kisses, but now that he was back, and with where his mind wandered during the blowjob, he didn't want Grant to have even the slightest hint of what he'd done.

Grant's eyelids twitched. "Are you…okay?"

"I'm fine. More than fine. But now, I need a shower." Jake shouldered past him on the narrow staircase. Grant's body felt hard and muscled beneath that brief touch. His cock stirred as he marched up the stairs, remembering Grant's fine body from their aborted bathroom encounter.

Chapter Six

JAKE SHOVED THE BUCKET FULL OF cleaning supplies into the closet. The common area was now thoroughly mopped and dusted for the morning rush. He headed into the kitchen and washed up—he could get an early start on the scones and do the bathrooms and take it easy for the rest of his shift.

In the kitchen, he turned on the radio and rummaged through the cupboards for the big metal bowl. It was in a different place almost every time he went searching for it. When Jake finally found it, he breathed a sigh of relief to find it clean this time.

Jake then rummaged through the locked staff food cupboard for the box of scone mix, flipped it open, and dumped the rest of the contents in the bowl. He added water and searched through the cupboards for the baking pans.

A throat cleared behind Jake, startling him.

"Sorry," the man said, immediately, as Jake turned around.

Oh, it's you. "I didn't hear you come in." Jake turned back to the bowl and dug his fingers in the dough.

"Listen," Grant said, his voice growing nearer, "I wanted to apologize."

"Apologize for what?"

"For...you know..."

"For being a dick?"

Grant chuckled. "I guess that's one way of putting it."

"You've said your apologies, so goodnight." Jake kneaded the dough with more force than normal.

When Grant didn't say anything and Jake didn't hear any retreating footsteps, Jake glanced over his shoulder. "Something else you want?"

"Can we talk about what happened?"

"What's to talk about? We wanted different things—I wanted a quickie, you wanted a hot and heavy make-out session—so we parted ways."

"A kiss is hardly a make-out session." There was defiance in his tone.

Jake felt his anger stirring. Before he said something he'd regret, he clamped his lips shut and took a deep breath. When he'd calmed enough, he said, "Let's not get into this again."

"Agreed." He leaned against the counter next to Jake. Grant wore a white T-shirt and another pair of gray boxer briefs…with a rather pronounced bulge in the front.

Damn it! No matter how furious he was, his dick had a mind of its own. It quickly swelled as it filled with blood.

When Jake didn't say anything, Grant said, "So what did you do today? You were gone for quite a while."

"Keeping an eye on my movements?" Jake asked, with the slightest tease in his voice. With the blood rushing to his groin, he had no energy to remain furious.

"It's a small hostel in a small town. I notice things."

"I went over to Inverness. Spent a few hours there."

"Ah, in search of Nessie? You really need to go to Drumnadrochit if you want a chance of catching a glimpse of the monster."

Jake smiled and refrained from making his immediate retort, something about the monster cocks he saw in the town. "I just needed some alone time in a different city." When the silence between them grew long, Jake asked, "And you? What did you do today?"

"I went for a jog up the road and back, hung out here and read for a bit, and did some research and made plans for a road trip I want to take Friday."

"Oh?"

"Yeah, it's been years since I've been to Skye—so I'm renting a car to go driving through the countryside, maybe stop in Portree for lunch."

"Sounds nice. Sounds boring, actually, but I know most people would think it sounds nice."

Grant rolled his eyes. "You really need to experience what the island has to offer. There are landscapes not found anywhere else in the world."

Jake chuckled. "Yeah, it's definitely different from home."

Grant tilted his head. "And what's home like? You said you're from Canada, right?"

"Yeah. You know any of the provinces?"

Grant scratched his chin. "I know Toronto."

Jake laughed again. "Everyone knows Toronto, but that's a city. The province I'm from is called Saskatchewan. My town is a small one-horse hick-town that no one's ever heard of. Anyway, it's flat."

"Flat?" Grant shook his head slightly. "I don't understand."

"I know—unless you're from Saskatchewan, you can't picture it. I honestly get that same reaction all the time here in Scotland. See this countertop? Imagine the land being that flat for as far as the eye can see. That's Saskatchewan."

"Sounds exotic."

Jake guffawed. "Maybe to you."

Grant smiled and bit his lip.

"What?"

He watched Jake for a long moment before answering. "You're cute when you're happy."

Jake rolled his eyes. "Thanks, I guess." He pulled his hands out of the dough and went to wash them.

"What's this?"

"Hmm?" Jake looked back. Grant picked something up off the floor.

"This fell out of your back pocket." Grant read from a small piece of paper, "The Brawny Scot."

Jake's heart thudded and ice coursed through his veins. He'd gone there as an eff-you to Grant, but hadn't actually wanted him to know about it. And, truthfully, as the hours passed, he'd grown regretful over going.

"Is that where you were today?" Grant's voice was low and quiet. There was an intensity in his eyes that Jake had seen only once before—during the previous night and their argument over kisses. Obviously, he knew what The Brawny Scot was.

"So what if I was?" Jake dried his hands with a towel and leaned against the counter, crossing his arms in front of him. He might regret his choices, but he wasn't going to apologize for them.

"You went to a fucking *sauna*?"

Jake took a deep breath, deciding which way to go with this. When the heat of anger warmed his cheeks, he had his answer. "Yes, I went. I sucked five dicks and got totally covered in cum." His words were quick and crisp, though muted so as to not wake anyone.

Grant shook his head. "Do you have no self-respect? No self-love?"

"What the *hell* are you talking about?"

"This!" Grant threw the card down on the counter, the oiled-up torso emblazoned across it shone in the kitchen's light. "Sex with no intimacy, blowjobs with no kissing, sucking anonymous dicks in the dark—it shows you don't respect yourself, that you just want to be used by some random man as a tool to get off. And this…this random sauna thing is fucking dangerous! Do you know how many diseases run rampant through there?"

Jake breathed in and out, trying to calm the anger that threatened to erupt. His face felt warm; he knew his cheeks were beet red. "Not all of us want boyfriends. Some of us just want sex. Hookups are fun, and if you think that only self-haters do them and they're always destructive, then you're living in some sort of dream world. Welcome to reality, Grant, people fuck strangers all the time."

Grant squeezed the bridge of his nose and closed his eyes. When he opened them, Jake could tell a lot of the man's anger had deflated. "That's not exactly what I'm saying."

"Then what are you saying, exactly?"

"Kissing adds passion and energy to sex—even anonymous sex. Your refusal to kiss me the other night would have made the blowjob mechanical. If I want mechanical, I'll use my fist. The motions are only half of sex—kissing and intimacy, however fleeting, are the other half."

"You need to grow up and separate sex from love. No one at the sauna wants a kiss, they just want to get off."

"Well, maybe that's the sauna culture. I have hookups now and then, but I always kiss—it makes a connection special, even if it's just for a moment and I don't know the guy's name."

Jake glared at him. As much as he wanted to remain mad at him, he felt his anger shrinking. "Why can't you accept that I just don't want to kiss?"

"Because in your case, Jake, I sense that it's something deeper. It's not just about not wanting to kiss."

Jake blinked, bewildered. "What the hell are you talking about?"

"Have you ever kissed a man?"

"Of course I have." A chasm opened up inside of him, an emptiness and yearning.

Grant squinted at him. "I mean *really* kissed a man…deep, hard, hungry."

He shifted positions. "What are you getting at, Grant?"

"Have you ever been intimate with a man? I mean, so close your heartbeats sync up?"

Peter. Jake slammed that chasm closed. "I told you, I'm not looking for love. I'm just looking for fucks."

"And have you ever been in love?"

"Fuck you." Jake's reaction had come before he could control his mouth. "Take your fucking judgmental crap and shove it up your fucking ass." Jake turned back to the scones, grabbing a couple spoons out of a drawer and shoved it closed with a loud clatter. He scooped the dough onto baking sheets.

"Jake…"

"Fuck off. Go to bed. You made your point."

"I'm sor—"

"I said, fuck off." Jake refused to turn and watch the man leave. Otherwise, Grant might see the unshed tears that stung Jake's eyes.

When the kitchen door finally closed and he was alone, Jake put his hand to his face and leaned on the counter. He fought to regain control.

Jake took a long shuddering breath and stood upright again. Tears no longer threatened to fall, but he felt emotionally drained. Empty. Tired.

Jake scooped the rest of the scones onto the baking sheets and shoved them in the oven. When they were baked and cooling on a rack, he emerged into the darkened common area, lit only by a handful of night-lights. He sat down in the dark.

He'd done everything but the bathrooms, he'd get hell for not doing them, but it didn't matter. Jake couldn't bring himself to stand up. Grant's words echoed in his mind. *Have you ever been in love?*

Jake's chest ached with a long-denied yearning.

Chapter Seven

Tuesday, 2:07 PM

JAKE STUMBLED DOWN THE LAST FEW stairs into the common room, laptop under his arm, glancing around to ensure Grant was nowhere in sight before proceeding through to the front desk. It, too, was mercifully empty, with the exception of Audra watching yet more videos.

"You look like hell," she said as he ambled to a stop in front of her and put his laptop on the counter.

"Thanks."

"Pleasure." She returned her focus to the video, something he barely heard the soundtrack to.

Jake stuck out his tongue. "I couldn't sleep. Tossed and turned." He looked down the hallway to the common room again. "You see that Grant guy around today?"

"I think he went for a hike or something." She blinked and then raised her eyebrows. "Why? Do you…like him?"

Jake opened his mouth, but before he could say anything, she gasped. "Oh, you're in love!"

"No!" he said, perhaps too sternly. "No…no, I'm not. We had an argument last night and I'd rather not see or talk to him right now."

"Ooo…lovers' spat…"

"We're not fucking lovers!" Jake closed his eyes, regretting his words.

"Wow," Audra said, barely more than a whisper.

"Sorry. I'm sorry. Like I said, no sleep and an argument to boot. I'm sorry."

She waved her hand. "No worries, mate."

Jake rested his elbows on the counter and his head in his hands. "And it's Tuesday." He closed his eyes, trying to shut out the world. But try as he might, all that filled his mind was last night's argument. *Have you ever been in love?*

With a heavy sigh, Jake lifted his head to find Audra staring at him.

"Hey," she said, "you know you can talk to me if something's bothering you, right?"

He nodded. "Thanks. I think I'll be okay, though." He pursed his lips and stood up straight. "Time for the weekly chore."

A sympathetic smile tugged at the corner of her lips. "Calling home?"

"Calling home." Jake picked up his laptop and plodded back into the empty common room. Sitting down in a corner, he fired up the computer and logged into video chat. It was about 8:30 AM back in Saskatchewan. His mother worked from home and his father had Tuesdays off, so this had very quickly become a part of their routine. Though he loved his parents, their continual pleas for him to come back home had quickly grown tiring.

The icon next to his mom's account turned from red to green. Holding back a sigh, he double-clicked on her name and waited for her to connect. Moments later, a large video window popped up on his screen with a surprisingly clear and smooth display.

"Hi, dear," she said, her voice slightly tinny.

"Hi, Mom." Jake made sure to put on his happy face. She was stressed enough with him being so far away for so long, she didn't need to worry about his happiness right now.

His mom looked somewhere off-screen. "Frank! Jake's on the computer!" she shouted. Jake reflexively tensed. Things were not good between him and his father and they hadn't been for a very long time. "How are things?" Her voice was tight, like every other time he called home.

"They're fine."

"Are you coming home soon?"

"I don't have a date planned yet, Mom. I'll let you know when I do."

It seemed like she wanted to say more, but something off-screen caught her attention and she kept her opinion quiet.

"Jake," his father said as he sat down next to his mom, his name coming out as little more than a grunt.

"Hi."

His mom narrowed her eyes. "Are you sure you're okay, Jake? You look exhausted. Are you still on the graveyard shift?"

"Yeah, yeah, I'm fine. Don't worry." He smiled, but doubted it appeared genuine.

There was a crinkle to his mother's forehead that told him she didn't believe a word he said. Thankfully, she let the topic slide, though he knew she'd be following up next week. "I ran into Peter yesterday."

Jake's heart fluttered. "Oh, yeah? How's he doing?"

"He says he's well. He's planning to go back to university, maybe get a masters in something." Another odd crinkle formed on his mother's forehead, but not one of concern. "He says you never write to him or call him. I think he misses you."

His heart fluttered some more, a yearning filled his gut. "Yeah, I, uh, haven't had time. I'll make sure to drop him a line soon." Jake hoped they didn't pick up on the quiver he heard in his voice.

"I hope you come home soon, dear, we all miss you."

"I miss everyone too, Mom."

A ringing phone interrupted his mother's next words. She excused herself and got up to answer it, leaving Jake alone with his father. Jake could sense his discomfort across the thousands of miles between here and home.

"So," his father said, sounding as awkward as Jake felt, "staying out of trouble?"

"For the most part," Jake said. Silence invaded and they stared at each other for far too long without saying a word. His father's gaze drifted, following something Jake couldn't see—most likely his mom wandering with the phone in her hand.

His father's eyes searched the screen, visibly struggling for something to say. "Keeping up with your piano?"

"Yup." Jake didn't know how much longer he could keep talking to his father. *Hopefully, Mom won't be on the phone for too long.* "I still perform at the local pub once a week...still go there every once in a while to just play around."

His father struggled again to come up with something to say. Eventually, they just stared at each other across the thousands of miles. He was obviously as uncomfortable as Jake felt, and the longer they stared, the more his anger bubbled up inside of him. He held it down, contained it, waiting for the moment his mom came back to break the tension.

Jake could remember when he and his father were like best of friends, doing guy stuff every weekend—fixing a car, going fishing, doing home repairs, and more. That all stopped years ago. Their relationship turned to ice pretty much the day he came out as gay. Ice...or fire. More often than not, their father-son problems turned into arguments rather than silence.

His father's eyes shifted from side to side, watching his mom wander back and forth with the phone. He opened his mouth to speak, but came out with no words. His chest sagged. Eventually, his father gave it another try. "So…" pausing, as if waiting for a sentence for form in his head, "are the girls in Scotland prettier than here in Canada?"

Jake closed his eyes briefly, the pressures and anger from last night roiled anew, stirred up by this. *Have you ever kissed a man?* Fleeting images of passionate embraces with Peter passed before his eyes. "You know I'm gay. How many times do we have to have this conversation?" He tried to keep the edge off of his words, but knew they still cut deep. Today was not the day to deal with this *yet again.*

His father's chest deflated further and his shoulders sagged. Suddenly, he appeared very old to Jake. "I know."

Have you ever been in love? A rush of emotions welled up behind Jake's eyes, difficult to contain. "Then why won't you ever accept it? When will you accept me?" He instantly wished he could take back his words; this was about Grant and Peter, not his father.

"I do accept you," he said, but the way his eyes avoided Jake spoke otherwise.

"No, you don't. Ever since I came out, you've treated me like I'm one big disappointment to you."

His father's gaze hardened and locked onto the screen. "Don't ever say that. You are *not* a disappointment."

"Yeah, well it doesn't fucking feel like it."

"Jake, you are my son, and I won't—"

Jake leaned forward and shoved his finger at the screen. "If I'm your son, then start treating me like your son!"

Frank's face went dark red. "How dare you!"

Jake leapt to his feet. "How dare I? How dare you! You've done nothing but treat me like a second class citizen since the day I came out!" *Have you ever been in love?*

Frank quickly rose to his feet too, leaning close to the webcam. Jake's screen was filled with his father's angry eyes. A vein stood out and pulsed on that red forehead. "I've done nothing but love and respect you. If you can't see that, then that's your own damn fault."

"If that's your idea of love, then I don't want your love."

Tears welled up in Jake's eyes. Wouldn't that top it off? Make the gay boy cry like a girl.

Jake grabbed the lid of his laptop and slammed it down. The tinny voice of his mom pleading for calm was sharply cut off.

His vision blurred with unshed tears as he looked around. Three people had wandered in, stood there and stared at him. One of them was Grant. "Fuck," Jake muttered.

He rushed across the room and through the gathered people, shoving Grant aside with far more force than intended. Rivulets ran down his cheeks as he crashed the door open and ran out into the gloomy day.

He ran to the only place he could get away from people, the only place that brought him any solace and peace in this land so far from home. Jake quickly reached the edge of the tiny town and clambered up the hill to the ruins overlooking the water.

He collapsed against a half-standing wall and dug the heels of his palms into his eyes, trying to stop the flow. His breath came in ragged, shuddering gasps as he slowly regained control of himself. Jake wiped his face one more time with his hands, grubby from the frantic scramble up the hill.

He took a deep breath and leaned his head back against the ancient stone, allowing the sound of lapping waves to fill the silence. Sniffling once more, he opened his eyes and watched the boats drift idly through the channel.

He replayed through the entire confrontation with his dad—it was bad, very bad. They'd had their differences over the years, but it had never exploded like that. *And it wasn't even about him.* Jake angrily swiped away a few more tears. *Well, it was partly about him. He's the root of it all.*

And Grant... Jake grimaced. *Of all the people to witness that meltdown...*

He gently hit the back of his head against the wall. "Fucking Grant. Fucking, fucking Grant. He needs to mind his own fucking business."

The rustle of pant legs against shrubbery made his blood run cold. He didn't have to turn his head to know who it was.

"Leave me alone, Grant."

A pair of legs wandered into Jake's peripheral vision. They didn't move away. Instead, Grant crouched down and looked at Jake, examining him.

"Are you okay?"

Jake rolled his head to the side, meeting Grant's eyes. "What the fuck do you think?"

Grant sat next to Jake, staring out at the water. "That's what I thought."

"I told you to go away." There was no anger behind his words anymore. Jake wasn't sure if he actually wanted Grant to leave him alone.

"And, yet, I'm still here." There was no challenge in his voice, either. It was as if they both just accepted that things were as they were.

Jake watched a gull soar through the air, coming to a graceful landing on a fishing boat. It squawked loud enough to be heard halfway across the water.

"Okay," Jake said, sniffling, "out with it."

"Out with what?"

"Whatever it is that you came out here to say. I should be more understanding of my father or I should be less confrontational or whatever pop psychology you're about to regurgitate. Or are you still harping on my lack of self-love?" Normally, Jake knew he'd say those words with heat and anger. Right now, he just felt defeated, self-pitying.

"I wasn't going to say anything. That's not why I followed you here."

"Then why did you follow me?"

Grant looked at him, care filling his gaze. He lifted his arm and wrapped it around Jake's shoulders. Any other time, any other day, he would have resisted such contact.

Today, Jake melted into Grant's body. He shifted his body down so he could rest his head on Grant's firm and muscled chest and wrap his arms around Grant's dangling forearm. Jake didn't know how long they lay there, but he watched a small fishing boat make its way down the channel, returning from some expedition out at sea. A loud chorus of gulls followed the boat.

"Do you get along with your family?" Jake asked, breaking the silence that had settled comfortably around them.

"No." He could feel tension in Grant's chest; it was no longer as soft to lean against. "I still talk to my sister, but not to my parents. It's their choice, not mine."

"Would you?" Jake asked, almost a whisper.

"Would I what?"

"If you had the chance to talk to them again, to get back that relationship...would you?"

"Yes," Grant said without hesitation. "When they first cut me off, I didn't care. I was done with it and done with them. But sometimes you don't know what you have until you no longer have it. You don't realize how important some relationships are until they're gone."

Jake didn't respond, didn't know how. Instead, they watched the gulls circle around a returning fishing boat.

As the rush of emotions from his call home faded, they were replaced by an unsettled feeling. This closeness…it wasn't comfortable. It wasn't what he wanted. Jake shifted his position, loosening his grip on Grant and instead hugging his arms to his chest.

"Hey." Grant pulled Jake into a tighter one-armed hug. "You okay?"

Jake sat upright, sitting beside Grant rather than leaning on him. "I'll be okay."

Grant looked him, scrutinizing. Suddenly, Grant's stomach growled loudly.

Jake smiled with an up-tick of his lips. "Sounds like you're hungry."

"I'm famished. Want to go to one of the pubs? My treat."

"No, I'm going to stay here for a bit."

Grant's eyes narrowed again as he considered something. "Do you want me to stay here with you a bit longer?"

"No," Jake said, immediately. "I need some alone time."

Grant nodded and faced the water once more. He got to his knees and leaned in to kiss Jake on the forehead.

Before his lips could make contact, Jake angled back, far out of reach.

"I see," Grant said, disappointed.

Jake kept his mouth shut, hoping Grant would take the hint and leave. Instead, Grant stood on his hands and knees, staring into Jake's eyes, both of them frozen in tableau. Eventually, he sat down on his haunches.

"I don't want you to think I came up here just to break you down and kiss you."

Jake brought his knees to his chest and rested the side of his head on his kneecaps, facing away from Grant. He refused to have this conversation right now. Eventually, he heard the rustle of Grant standing and passing through the overgrown weeds and down the hill. Jake turned his head in the other direction, to watch Grant's retreating back. Tears pooled in the corners of Jake's eyes, spilling sideways down his face and splattering on his knees.

Tuesday, 10:23 PM

Jake's fingers moved over the ivory keys with a languid fluidity that came from years of knowing the instrument intimately. Half-lidded, his eyes were unfocused, staring into nowhere, staring into the past.

It was a tune of his own making, a melody that came to him over the past year. It changed every time he played it, his emotions feeding into the sound, the tempo, and the progression of notes. The noise around him, the other patrons in the pub, few as they were, faded to nothing as he cocooned himself in the music. The notes became his comfort.

Some time later, Jake sensed a presence. He opened his eyes, almost dreading to find Grant there. Thankfully, it wasn't him.

"I don't know much about music, but even I can tell when someone is hurting." Samantha, the soft-spoken matron of the pub, rested an arm on the top of the upright piano, concern clearly written on her features.

Jake glanced around behind him. The pub was empty except for Samantha's husband, Andrew, behind the bar, wiping down the fixtures.

"Is it 10:30 already?" The pub closed early on Mondays and Tuesdays.

Samantha nodded. "Rough day?"

Jake eased the cover down over the keys. "You don't know the half of it."

"Would you like to talk about it?"

"No," Jake said, too quickly. "Sorry. No."

She looked as if she was considering something. She scooched him over and sat beside him on the bench. "I don't know if I ever told you, but I don't get along with my parents. It took me a long time to make peace with it. I still talk with them, visit them on holidays, see them occasionally throughout the year, but we really don't get on well. I can just never measure up to what they seem to want from me."

Jake closed his eyes briefly, having put together the pieces. "Grant was here, wasn't he?"

"He was. He's concerned about you, asked if we knew you. But I'm not done telling you about my parents." Before he could reply, she continued. "This rocky relationship devastated me for a long time. I was never happy. And then I realized that I need to live my life for myself and not measure up to other people's expectations. I don't suspect my parents were happy with that, but we've reached some form of compromise. And, truly, I'm glad I didn't cut them out of my life. I would have really regretted it."

Jake rubbed his eyes. He was weary and exhausted, and only a half hour from starting his shift.

"It's a little more complicated than that," he said, finally, his voice as soft as hers.

"It always is. But the message is still the same: Don't throw them away."

He ran his fingers along the polished wood of the piano, avoiding her eyes. The room got suddenly darker as Andrew shut off a few of the lights. Still, Samantha didn't ask him to leave, so he sat.

"Tell me about the music," she said.

He finally looked up at her, then back at the piano. "I don't know, it's some tune in my head. I can't get it out, so I play it. Whenever I'm in here, I play some sort of variation on the same thing."

"I know." She nodded gently. "It normally has a feeling of longing to it, but today was different. Today, it felt...regretful...wistful."

"Yeah," he muttered.

"Is it...is it a song *for* someone?"

"Maybe. Yeah. Yeah, it is."

She skimmed her fingers along the edge of the piano and then looked at Jake again. "I watched you for a few minutes before you quit. You were completely immersed in it."

"I find...I find it helps me. When I play music from the heart like that, it helps me...I don't know...helps me process things. It helps me figure things out."

"And did today help?"

Jake shrugged. "I don't know. There's a lot going on. I think it helped me just put some things aside, even just for half an hour."

She put a hand on his arm. "I'm glad, Jake. Remember, if you ever want to talk about something, I'm here."

"Thanks, Samantha." He glanced at the clock on the wall. "I gotta go. Thanks for letting me hang out for a bit—I needed the time and space."

She saw him out the door and he walked through the chilled night air to the hostel, watching the stars as he traversed the streets.

Chapter Eight

JAKE HUMMED ALONG TO THE RADIO AS he pulled out a fresh box of biscuit mix and poured it into the bowl with some water. He stopped his fingers before they dug into the bowl. He'd had visitors at this point every night for the last four nights.

He turned around, expecting someone there, but found no one. He abandoned the bowl and quietly stepped out of the kitchen and across the building to the stairwell, listening for the telltale creak of floorboards. All seemed quiet.

Still, Jake wasn't ready to dive into the mix. He'd give it five minutes or so, to see if anyone ended up coming down. He turned off the radio, crossed his arms and leaned a hip against the countertop, watching the door.

Sure enough, the creak of stairs broke the silence. Someone was on his way down.

Did he want to suck dick today? Jake wasn't sure.

A good blowjob might get his mind off things, get him back on track. He still hadn't decided if he wanted to suck or not by the time the door swung open. A stocky man, a couple years older than Jake, shorter and with much more muscle, entered. He had a pug nose and close-cropped black hair, and wore a pair of dark boxers and a tight white T-shirt, stretched across his broad chest. Jake didn't recognize him.

"Are you Jake?" His accent sounded American.

"Yeah." He scratched his cheek, attempting to appear casual. "What can I do for you?"

"I need some help...relieving some tension."

Jake managed to refrain from rolling his eyes. *We're going with porn dialogue here, apparently.*

"I see," said Jake, ambling forward, giving the man what he wanted. "Perhaps I can help with that." He groped the man through the front of his boxers. The man was reasonably gifted below the waist.

The man stared at him. The glint in his eyes made it clear he enjoyed this, but his face gave no other outward sign.

Jake got down on his knees and pulled the man's boxers down, his hard uncut dick flopping with the movement. His balls were held tight against the base of his cock, and all of it was nestled in a wild mess of hair. Jake wrapped his fingers around the base of the man's cock and looked up at the man, searching.

"Take it, punk, swallow my sausage." The man's voice was low and gritty.

If Jake were watching this on his laptop, he probably would have burst out laughing at the shitty dialogue. Instead, he focused on the slit in front of his face, a small drop of precum forming and expanding. Jake licked it up, brushing the tip of his tongue across the man's slit, eliciting a shudder.

Jake slid his tongue over the man's head, driving it beneath the folds of foreskin. He circled his tongue, smoothing and stretching every crease and wrinkled skin. Pulling the excess skin into his mouth, he tugged, giving it a gentle stretch. The man's hand fell on top of Jake's head, holding tight.

He released the skin from his mouth, then ran his tongue around the head again, pulling a new wad of skin into his mouth and tugging back. Jake let go and stroked the man's cock, staring at it.

The last couple days tumbled through his mind, the events, the emotions, the words...*Have you ever kissed a man?* Suddenly, Jake got to his feet, staring into the other man's eyes, still stroking the man's dick. He looked back at Jake, confused, unsettled.

"On your knees, bitch," the man said, not sounding near as confident as he had moments ago.

The man was moderately attractive—not particularly beautiful, but not ugly, either. Jake had never really stopped to seriously consider the attractiveness of his hookups before. But things were different now.

"Are you gonna suck me or stare at me?"

The man was a bastard. They all were. But now it suddenly mattered. Or did it?

Have you ever kissed a man?

Jake had kissed a man before. Peter had been slow and gentle, the touching of their lips had stopped time. To kiss someone else would feel like betrayal. *Betrayal? I told him I didn't want him. Surely, he's moved on.* Jake had never kissed anyone else…could he?

The other man continued to stare at him questioningly.

Jake closed his eyes and leaned forward, reaching out with his lips, searching for contact. Two heavy hands landed on his chest and shoved him backward. He stumbled back several steps, catching himself on the counter before tumbling to the floor.

"What the fuck?" the man said, his voice loud, too loud.

"I…I just…I…"

"I'm not fucking *gay.*" The man still had his voice raised; he would wake people.

Jake put out his hands. "I'm sorry, I'm sorry, I just got carried away." He kept glancing at the door, expecting someone to barge in and make it worse.

The man stalked closer, his hands balled into fists. "Do I look like a fucking homo?"

Jake pressed hard against the counter, trying to get further away but failing. "No. No. I'm sorry."

The man's hand shot out and grabbed a handful of Jake's shirt, pulling him closer, nose to nose. "You know what I do to fags?" The man cocked his fist back; Jake watched it, trembling.

A voice intruded. A blessed, beautiful voice. "You know what I do to homophobes?"

The man let go of Jake and whirled around to face the new person. Jake stumbled back, catching himself on the edge of the counter.

"This is none of your fucking business," the man spat.

Grant rolled his eyes and crossed his arms. "Your cock is hanging out."

He quickly stuffed it back in his boxers. He raised a finger, but before he could say anything, Grant interrupted. "Get the fuck out of here."

The man looked back at Jake, face beet red, before stomping out. "Fags."

Jake, paralyzed with fear and not moving, watched Grant as he approached. When Grant laid a hand on Jake's shoulders, Jake's legs turned to jelly. He caught himself on the counter again before falling to the floor; Grant slung his arm around Jake, supporting him.

"Here, let's go sit down." Grant guided him through the door and to a chair in the darkened eating area. He let go of Jake and sat in the chair next to him. Jake already missed the comfort of that strong arm.

Grant leaned forward, elbows resting on his knees, watching Jake. The silence enveloped them and Jake took deep breaths, calming himself.

"Mind telling me what all that was about?" Thankfully, there was no accusation or judgment in Grant's voice.

"I'd rather not. Hookup gone bad, that's all."

Grant's eyes narrowed slightly, as if he knew Jake was concealing important details. "I figured as much, what with his cock hanging out and everything."

"You know, standard aborted hookup," Jake said, looking everywhere but at Grant. "He wanted me to blow him, he was a huge asshole, we parted ways."

"You left out the part where you almost had your lights punched out."

"What are you getting at?" Jake finally glared at Grant, then reigned in his anger.

"What I'm getting at," Grant said, as he put his hands on Jake's knees, "is that you're going to get yourself hurt one of these days—either by catching a disease or by meeting up with somebody like that thug."

"Like anyone would care." Jake's voice was low, a mere whisper.

Grant's warm hand found its way to Jake's cheek. "Hey. I care."

"Why?"

Grant blinked several times. "What do you mean 'why?'"

"Why do you care? It's not a hard question."

"I care because I like you. I think you're smart, good-looking, and have a lot to offer the world. I want the best for you, for you to be happy."

Jake wasn't sure what to say, wasn't sure if he could muster together a string of words. He stared down at Grant's chest, no longer able to look him in the eye. Grant's chest rose and fell with gentle breaths, hypnotic to Jake. The rhythm of breaths changed when Grant let out a yawn.

"You should go to bed," Jake said, still watching his chest.

"Are you going to be okay?"

"Yeah. I have work to do. I can't sit around all night."

They sat in silence for several moments more, Jake still not making eye contact.

"All right," Grant said, pushing himself to his feet, "I'll see you tomorrow?"

Jake looked up at him. "I live and work here, so I guess so."

"Goodnight, Jake."

"Night."

Jake watched Grant walk out of the room, his tight round ass encased in thin cotton. After that wonderful sight left the room, Jake got up and returned to making biscuits.

Chapter Nine

Wednesday, 3:57 PM

J AKE GRIPPED THE HANDRAIL AS HE ambled down the stairs. His heavy eyelids drooped. He reached the bottom and paused for a moment to gather himself. Yawning heavily, he made his way to the front desk and put his arms on the counter, rested his head, and closed his eyes.

"Morning, mate." For once, Audra was not annoyingly shrill or absurdly loud. But, like always, the faint, tinny sounds of an online video reached his ears. "What happened to you?"

"No sleep," Jake mumbled.

In what had to be a first-ever event, Jake heard Audra click the trackpad on the laptop to stop the video and then close the lid.

"Upset with your father?"

Jake crinkled his brow. "You overheard that?"

"I think the whole town overheard that, sweetie."

Jake sighed into the countertop. His father's word's echoed in his ears and his angry face on the screen flickered through his mind. "We used to get along just fine."

She patted his hand. When he eventually lifted his head and stood upright, she reached to the corkboard on the wall and grabbed two slips of paper.

"I have two messages for you." She handed him the notes. "Your mother called; she wants to talk to you. And Grant is looking for you." A lilt entered her voice at the mention of Grant's name.

Jake glanced them over, then crumpled them both and tossed them in the basket behind Audra. "Thanks," he muttered and wandered in the direction of the kitchen. Before reaching the door, the tinny sound of another web video reached his ears.

He shambled toward the fridge and rested his hand against it, almost too tired to open it. The metal door was covered in postcards from travelers who had passed through. Some were from far-off places like South America, Australia, and Japan, but most were from within Europe, probably from tourists hopping from country to country, drinking their way through the continent.

Jake had been in Scotland for almost a whole year now, with nearly all of that time spent in Kyleakin or Inverness. Europe was at his doorstep, dozens of countries a short plane hop away, and he'd wasted his time scrubbing toilets in this godforsaken town. All the clubs and saunas were hours away. Kyleakin was no place for a horny, young twink like him.

Neither was Saskatchewan.

"Fuck." He opened the fridge and pulled out his bread, popping two slices in the toaster.

Jake had to go somewhere—he had to get far away from here and even further away from home. *Home. Fuck. I have no home.*

He threw the bread back in the fridge and scanned through the postcards once more. He mentally crossed out most of them as either places that were too expensive or probably not gay-friendly. One postcard with dented corners caught his attention; he slid the magnet off and brought it out from among the mass of global destinations.

A city, or at least part of a city, filled with stone buildings and red tile roofs, all surrounded by a massive smooth stone wall, jutted into a brilliant blue body of water. "Dubrovnik." Jake flipped the postcard over. "Croatia. Hmm."

Jake slipped the postcard into his back pocket and returned to his toast. He slathered it with Nutella, distracted with thoughts of Croatia. From what he'd heard, it was fairly gay-friendly. Could he do another year away from home? *Fuck, there's nothing at home anyway. Home is just a word.*

He tossed his knife in the sink to wash later and walked through the door to the eating area.

Coincidentally, almost as if there were a higher power at work, a dog-eared copy of a Europe travel guide sat abandoned on one of the tables. In a matter of seconds, Jake had the book open to Dubrovnik and read as he munched on his toast.

Wednesday, 6:50 p.m.

A cold breeze blew across the water up to the hill, reaching Jake as he sat against Dunakin Castle. The squawk of gulls was the only sound on an otherwise quiet evening. In his lap, his leather-bound notebook sat open. Poetry had long been abandoned, but his page was filled with carefully written words.

> *Dear Peter,*
>
> *How have you been? I miss talking to you. Yes, I know I'm half to blame for that.*
>
> *My mom says you've been asking about me lately. I wanted to let you know I'm well and wanted to let you know that I won't be coming back to Canada for another year. I'm enjoying life over here in Europe and want to spend more time here while I can. I'm going to look at spending the next year in Croatia, preferably in Dubrovnik.*
>
> *You should come visit me. I would like that a lot. I miss you.*
>
> *I miss your smile and your laugh. I miss your company.*

I haven't told my parents yet that I'm not coming back. I guess by the time you read this, they'll know. And I suspect they'll tell you and you'll probably already know. But I wanted you to hear it from me.

I know I already said it, but I'll say it again: You should come visit me.

Once I get settled, I'd like to show you around Dubrovnik and spend time with you.

Sincerely,

Jake

Writing had been half the battle. Months had gone by of struggling to write. This was the first complete letter he'd written. The big challenge now was to actually mail it.

Jake closed his notebook and tucked the pen inside. Mailing it could be done later.

He closed his eyes and absorbed the sounds of the waves and gulls, the smell of the salt water, and the kiss of cool air on his cheek. His insides felt unsettled, but he couldn't tell if it was fear over making a mistake or excitement over choosing the right thing.

Dubrovnik will be good. I'll thrive there. I'll enjoy life.

He had to keep repeating those words to himself, a personal mantra.

Problem was, he didn't think it was helping.

Chapter Ten

MUFFINS COOLED ON THE RACKS IN the kitchen, their aroma filling the entire main floor of the hostel. The washrooms, both toilets and showers, were sparkling from the main floor to the attic. The main floor was vacuumed and all other chores were done. Now he just had to hang out for a few more hours, keeping an eye on things in case something unexpected happened in this slow, dreary, predictable town. He sat in an easy chair in the lobby, a pale lamp feebly keeping the darkness at bay.

Fuck, I'm horny.

No one had come down to utilize his midnight services. With yesterday's disastrous blowjob and all the other stuff, it had been something like sixty hours since he'd last had cock. He smiled, thinking of the last blowjob, of having that line-up of dicks at the glory hole.

His cock grew hard as his skin remembered the sensation of being cum-covered, dripping and sticky with the loads of other men. Jake dropped his hand down to his crotch and slowly rubbed as he viscerally remembered the texture and taste of each cock as it slid past his lips and deep into his mouth.

Already, Jake's cock ached with a deep-seated need for release. He paused, listening for any sounds. From where the chair was placed, he couldn't see the stairs, but would be able to hear anyone coming down. All was silent.

Slowly, drawing out the moment, he unzipped his jeans and slipped his hard cock through the hole in his boxers. It stood proud and erect, hard and red. Jake spit into his hand and rubbed it over the head of his dick, making it shiny, wet, and slick. He slid down in his seat, stretching out across the cushion.

Jake stroked up and down his shaft, skimming his fingers over the head with every upstroke. With his other hand, he tugged his T-shirt up and flicked his nipples, then pinched and twisted them, the flicker of pain shooting straight to his cock. He gasped softly.

He brought his hand down and readjusted, popping his balls out from his boxers. He continued stroking, tugging his tight sack.

In his mind's eye, the men from the bathhouse were gone. In their place stood Grant in full Scottish kilt gear. He bent over, just like that first day in the kitchen. The hem of his kilt rose as the fabric slid over his luscious, round ass. Jake closed his eyes, focusing on the mental image of Grant bent over, ass in the air.

He imagined sliding his hand along that taut curve, pulling the kilt up the rest of the way and revealing bare, hairy cheeks. Jake wanted to lick it, to taste it, to probe it. He pressed his body close against the Scot, his cock firm in the man's ass crack. Jake reached around, fondling under the front of the man's kilt, playing with a huge, dripping cock. He grasped it and…

Jake's body shuddered and the fantasy evaporated as climax hit him hard. He grunted and shot a thick load over his stomach, creating a deep pool just above his belly button. He gasped and struggled to catch his breath and clear the stupor in his mind.

Sated and calmed, he tucked his cock and balls back in his boxers and zipped up his jeans. Carefully, Jake cleaned the cum from his stomach, puddling his load in his hand. With his stomach mostly clean, he tugged down his shirt and stood to take his load in the toilet and wash his hands.

A creak on the stairs broke the silence. Soft footsteps followed. Someone was coming.

Jake eyed the cum in his hand, then the stairs, and then the direction to the bathroom. There was no way he'd get there in time. He'd be caught cum-handed.

Heart beating furiously, Jake did the only thing he could think of. He put his lips to his hand and tilted his head backward. His entire load, tart and sour, slipped over his tongue and into his mouth. He swallowed, downing everything, then furiously licked his palm clean.

He dried his hand on the inside of his shirt just as someone came down the last few steps to the common room.

Jake licked his lips and tried not to look guilty as the person took the last step down. He relaxed when he saw who it was.

"Grant."

Grant's eyebrow ticked up. "Why do you sound so relieved?"

"Never mind." Jake felt the tightness of drying cum on the palm of his hand and across his bottom lip. He hoped there was nothing visible. At least the lighting was low. "What's up?" *You're obviously not here for a blowjob.*

Grant walked past him and sat down heavily in the chair Jake had just vacated. He wore only a pair of loose gray boxer briefs. His chest and tight stomach had a light sprinkle of dark hair, enough to give him a thoroughly masculine appearance. The light glimmered in the short hairs and cast shadows under his pointed nipples.

Jake stood and watched him until Grant gave him a questioning look, then sat on the end of the sofa nearest to Grant.

"I just wanted to talk to you," Grant said. "I tried to catch you during the day but we just didn't seem to cross paths."

"I wasn't in the mood for talking to people."

"I see. But you're talking to me now…"

Jake didn't answer, unsure if he wanted Grant to go to bed or stay here for a while. He'd let Grant decide.

"How are you?"

"My tenuous relationship with my parents blew up a day and a half ago. I have no home. How do you think I am?" Jake wasn't able to reign in his bitterness.

"You have a home," Grant corrected him.

"Technically, I have a house to go back to. If a home is a place where you feel safe and welcome, then, no, I don't have a home. My father has been uncomfortable with me since the day I came out and it's just gotten worse since then." Jake leaned back on the couch, resting his head and staring up at the black ceiling.

Silence settled between them and separated them. Each moment made the distance wider. Eventually, Jake said, "I'm moving to Croatia."

"Interesting."

Jake righted himself and looked at Grant. "What do you mean by 'interesting?'"

"Why aren't you going home?"

"I told you already, I don't have a home," Jake snapped.

"You know what I mean. Why aren't you going back to Canada? Or, for that matter, why aren't you just staying here a little longer?"

"I need excitement. I need belonging."

Grant blinked several times, as if trying to parse Jake's statement. He started to say something, but stopped.

"What? Out with it." Jake crossed his arms over his chest.

He still didn't reply for several more moments. Grant stared at him, weighing, assessing. Eventually, he said, "How can you find belonging if you don't let anyone get close to you? You're looking for escape, not belonging."

Jake stood up and walked into a dark corner, staring out the window into the pitch-black night. He couldn't face Grant right now. "Fuck you."

He heard movement behind him, Grant getting up and walking. His voice came from just behind Jake. "You know what I mean. I see a lot of hurt and a lot of avoidance."

"This is the same thing you've been harping on for days now," Jake said, his words spilling out of him and his voice sounding harsh. "You're still pissed that I won't kiss you and you can't take no for an answer."

Grant exhaled sharply, as if biting back a reply. "This has nothing to do with your refusal to kiss me, specifically, but it has everything to do with what I've seen over the past few days. I see you searching for something, but unwilling to take the risk and go for it."

Jake turned around, arms across his chest again. "Oh, really, and what am I searching for?"

"That, I don't know. I'm not sure if you know either." Grant reached out and put a hand on Jake's shoulder. It warmed him, but he refused to acknowledge it.

Jake shrugged Grant's hand off his shoulder and turned back to the window. "You should go back to bed."

Behind him, Grant exhaled sharply, but his shuffling feet did take him back toward the stairs. When Jake was sure the man was gone, he switched off the lamp and sat in the darkness. "Fuck."

Chapter Eleven

Thursday, 4:20 PM

J AKE GLANCED AT THE CLOCK ON THE wall of the staff dorm. His mother had left numerous messages at the front desk and in his email, repeatedly asking him to be online for a video call at 10:30 AM, Saskatchewan time. Reluctantly, knowing she would persist until she succeeded, he agreed. In ten minutes it would be that time in Saskatchewan.

Rather than have a repeat of such a public meltdown like with the last video call, Jake had asked his co-workers to give him privacy in the attic. The room was quiet and dim, with four cots next to four nightstands and four lockers. Beside him, sunlight blazed through a small window with a lacy curtain, providing ample light for a webcam.

He had the program open, with his status set to "appear offline." His mother's face was framed in a small green box, indicating she was online. Online and waiting for him. He could still get out of it, send a message, saying something had come up. Or he could just avoid it—turn off the computer and walk away. She would persist, though. And, at some point, Jake had to tell her about moving to Croatia for a year before returning to Canada— so he might as well do it today. He didn't want to have that conversation, but knew it would get harder the longer he waited.

When the clock ticked over to 4:27, he moved his mouse over his own icon and let his finger hover above the trackpad, weighing his options again. Finally, Jake brought his fingers down and clicked, changing his status to "online".

Almost instantly, his speakers spit out a tune as his mom initiated a call. Heart thudding in his chest, so strongly he feared it would be visible on cam, he clicked on "connect".

His mother appeared, the video frame flickering and freezing several times before smoothing out.

"Jake? Are you there?" She peered into her screen, the bags under her eyes suddenly deepened and magnified with the angle of the light. She looked tired—she probably hadn't slept since that disastrous call. "Ah, I see you now!" She smiled, but he could tell there was some hurt there. More than usual.

"Yeah, I'm here. Hi, Mom." He put on a smile for her, but knew it probably looked as forced as hers.

"Thank you for letting me call you." She sometimes pulled out the trick of making him feel guilty as a way of cowing him into being agreeable. Normally, it might work. But not today.

"I've been wanting to talk to you about something—"

"Is that Jake?"

That was the voice he hadn't expected to hear. Moments later his father stepped into view and settled down next to his mother. His father didn't look at the screen and had a ball cap pulled low on his head, shadowing his eyes.

"What are you doing home?" Jake tried not to sound too distraught. He wanted a quick chat with his mother, to break the news to her, and then get on with his day. The last thing Jake wanted right now was to talk to his father.

His father looked at his mother, and she said, "I made him take the morning off."

Jake felt an ambush coming. This was a set-up of some sort.

"What's going on?"

She put her hand on his father's arm. "It's time that you two had a heart-to-heart."

Jake shook his head. "I don't think we're wanting that, mom."

His father stared in his lap, but his eyes glanced up at the screen when Jake spoke. There was a hurt there too, to a depth Jake had never seen in those eyes.

"This conversation is not optional, dear. You and your father have been distant for far too long."

"Yeah, well, I don't see how a conversation is going to change that."

His father looked up at him again, eyes again colored with hurt and pain. Jake furrowed his brow, confused.

"I love you, dear, but keep your mouth shut," his mom said.

Jake blinked rapidly, but kept his lips tight. He couldn't remember the last time his mother had scolded him. He glanced at his father, then back to her, waiting for the bombshell…or whatever this call was about.

"I know you *think* you have your dad figured out. I know you *think* he's homophobic, that he's uncomfortable with you being gay, but I assure you, you are wrong."

Jake looked at his father, then his mother, and back again, waiting for him to speak, waiting for something, anything. His father watched her, too. It appeared that she'd scolded him, as well.

She turned to her husband. "Frank?"

His father's gaze fell to his lap again before returning up at the screen. "When I was younger than you, son, and I was in high school, I became best friends with a boy by the name of Jake." His voice was quiet, but powerful, and his features were sad. Jake was held rapt. He'd never seen his father quite like this. "We were inseparable. In grade twelve, shortly before graduation, he told me a secret. Jake told me he was gay and had met a boy he liked. The admission changed nothing in our friendship. I still loved him as my best friend and we hung out regularly."

Jake ran that sentence through his head again. His father had never once mentioned having a gay friend.

"Will. Jake's partner was named Will. Jake and Will took off like wildfire—they fell in love deep and fast. And I didn't lose Jake, if anything, I gained a new friend in Will." Suddenly, his father's face brightened and a small smile touched his lips. He reached over and clasped his wife's hand. "In fact, it was Will who introduced me to your mom."

His mom smiled and rubbed his father's arm. He seemed to draw strength from that; he sat a little straighter and looked into the screen again.

Jake had never heard of Jake, this man who shared his name, or Will. He couldn't recall any of his parents' friends that had a name similar to that—or any friends that were in a same-sex relationship. If they were so close to Jake and Will, what happened?

His father's smile faded, replaced with a frown. Perhaps he was about to find out why the friendship ended.

"They were together happily for years. About a year and a half before you were born, Will was diagnosed with AIDS." His father's already quiet voice went quieter. Jake strained to hear, rapt on every word. "By the time he was diagnosed, it was already really bad. The doctors gave him six months to live."

His mother rubbed his back as his father took a deep breath. Jake was in shock. He'd never fathomed any of this as possible. He'd never heard even an inkling of this.

"Will held on for ten months. Jake took care of him every day and your mom and I did what we could—providing meals, helping around the house, visiting, emotional support…it wasn't just Jake that was losing family, it was all of us. The day Will died was one of the hardest days of my life.

"Being a small town, everyone knew what happened to Will. And, being a small town, everyone hated Jake and Will for bringing AIDS to their community—even though Jake was *not* HIV-positive. After Jake buried his partner, the attacks started. He'd be called names on the street, spit at. Someone spray-painted 'fag' all over his car. He got death threats in the mail."

"Oh my God," Jake said, words barely more than a whisper.

His father wiped his moist eyes. "Then they burned down his house."

"Did they ever catch the people who did all that?"

"No."

"We're pretty sure the police were part of the problem," his mother added. "They didn't want to protect someone they didn't feel belonged in their town."

"It gets worse, Jake." His father paused to take a deep, shuddering breath. "Someone followed through with their death threat. A month before you were born, someone broke into his place after midnight and shot him with a hunting rifle."

Jake brought his hand to his face, covering his mouth, struck with shock. He watched as a tear rolled down his father's cheek and his mother put her arm around him.

"Did they at least do something about that guy? Did they catch him?"

His father shook his head. "They caught him. Everyone knows who it was. But the police botched the evidence collection and it was all inadmissible in court. He got away with murder."

"Further proof the police were part of the problem," his mother added.

"When he died, we learned that none of his family wanted anything to do with the funeral. His parents had been somewhat accepting of him, but Will dying of AIDS pushed them away. Other than your mom and I, there were only about five people at the funeral—and finding a minister to perform the funeral and burial was a nightmare of its own. In the end, he left what little hadn't been destroyed to us. In the end, we were his only real family."

Jake felt a tear roll down his own cheek. "Was I…was I named after him?"

His mother nodded, her eyes glistening.

"Yeah," his father said. "And about a month after you were born, we knew we had to get out of there. We had your grandma take care of you for a week while your mom and I sold the house and left town. We couldn't live in a town that would allow such a thing to happen."

"Ideally, in a perfect world, we would have stayed and tried to change the people, to make them realize what they've done." His mother's voice was filled with hurt. "But that was a battle we were unprepared to fight. And if they had no problem with murdering an innocent man who had done nothing, how would they react to us, pushing for justice?"

"You had to leave—I understand. Those people weren't going to change. You had to leave for your own safety."

"And for your safety, Jake," his father said.

"Have you ever gone back?"

His father nodded, but it was his mother who spoke. "When you were about two, we got grandma to babysit you for the day and we went for a drive to visit Jake and Will's graves. It wasn't good.

"We were in and out of town in an hour. We didn't want to see anyone we knew. We didn't want to see the murderers—and as far as I'm concerned, they're *all* guilty. The headstones were kicked over, smashed, and spray-painted. We haven't gone back since. I can't see that again."

Jake sat in stunned silence, processing all he'd just learned. Of all the bombshells he could have thought were coming, this was not one of them. His parents watched him, both their faces wrought with relived grief.

"Why have I never heard this before?" It was an honest questioning, not an accusation.

"It was never an appropriate story when you were young, and then when you came out, we didn't want to fill your head with fear," his mother said. She looked at his dad and then back at Jake. "And as you can see, this experience still leaves us very raw."

Jake ran through the horrific events in his head. To know this happened to anyone was horrible enough, but to a close friend of his parents?

"So do you understand why I made your dad finally tell you this story?" she asked, pulling out the voice she used when he was a kid, the voice that told him there was a lesson to be learned here.

Jake watched at his dad, his pained face and the eyes still shadowed from his ball cap. "It's not homophobia that got between dad and I, it was the story of Jake and Will."

His dad took a deep breath, audibly inhaling through his nose. "I have absolutely zero problem with you being gay, Jake. What I let get in the way was fear. I've seen the very worst that one human being can do to another human being, for absolutely no reason other than what gender that person loves. Your mom and I lost friends—we lost family—to fear and hatred. I want you to be happy, I want you to love and be loved, but I'm terrified someone is going to hate you for it. I don't…I don't want to lose you, Jake. I apologize from the bottom of my heart for letting this tragedy from the past get in the way of me being a father to you. I didn't even fully realize what I was doing until your mom confronted me and sat me down." A smile ticked his lips upward. "You know how your mother is when she has a point she needs to make."

His mom slapped his father's shoulder.

Jake laughed, short and soft, bringing a small smile to his tear-streaked face.

"I love you, Jake. I truly do. You are exactly the son I've always wanted and you've done wonderful things in the memory of my friend Jake, without even being aware of it. He would be proud of you for how you've carried on his name."

Jake wiped the fresh tears from his face. "I love you too, Dad."

Chapter Twelve

Thursday 10:10 PM

JAKE'S FINGERS MOVED OVER THE PIANO with a speed and agility he didn't often possess. Some small part of him was conscious that the pub had largely emptied out, with fishermen having long gone to bed to prepare for an early morning. There weren't many late night pub-crawlers at the hostel this week.

Most of the day had been lost in a hazy tumult. After ending the conversation with his parents, Jake had wandered aimlessly up the road, toward the bridge. He got halfway over it before randomly deciding to turn around and head back to Dunakin Castle. How long he spent at the ruins, watching over the water, he didn't know. He'd carried his leather-bound notebook with him everywhere but didn't write anything. Somehow, sometime, he'd ended up here in the pub with a basket of fish and chips in front of him. And then he found himself at the piano.

Like last time, like always, like every time to come, the music wrapped around him, the notes became his language, and the melody became his story. What the music was saying, he didn't know. Jake sat, played, and let his subconscious move him.

A dainty hand lay across the top of the piano, pulling him from the cocoon of music. His fingers slowed and the notes tapered off. He looked up at Samantha, dressed impeccably with not a hair out of place, despite a busy dinner crowd a short while ago.

"Here we are again." She sat next to him.

"Do you play?"

"Oh, I used to, when I was a wee child. I doubt I remember much now. I used to play side-by-side with my dad." Her smile broadened into a grin. "Those were some of the happiest times of my childhood, years before my parents and I went our separate ways."

Jake's fingers moved again, breaking out into the old familiar tune of *Hot Cross Buns*. He looked at her and tried to put on his most mischievous smile as he continued to play. She inclined her head, smiled, and put her fingers to the keys. It started a bit choppy, but she soon caught on, keeping perfect time. As they cycled through the tune for the third time, Jake's fingers moved with wild abandon, bringing whimsical flourishes to the age-old tune. Samantha laughed with delight and the timing fell apart, the tune evolving into a discordant mishmash. Jake laughed along as the music died down.

"So when you were in here a few days ago, playing a melancholy tune…things have gotten better?"

"Oh, yes, absolutely. I still have a lot to…process, a lot to figure out."

She put an arm around his shoulders. "Life is never easy, is it?"

He chuckled. "No, it isn't."

"Grant was in here, searching for you."

"Yeah, I was kind of hard to find today. I needed to sort out a lot of stuff."

"Grant is a nice lad, isn't he? Cute. And caring. He seems to worry about you a lot."

Jake's fingers found the keys again, pressing down on a few random notes. "Yeah. I've been an ass with him all week—and all he's done is be nice to me."

"And why do you think that is?"

Jake looked down at his lap. "I don't know."

Her arm around his shoulder hugged him tight. "He probably sees the same thing I do—a wonderful young man who doesn't know how wonderful he is…and a man who seems to be carrying around far too much hurt."

Jake was still staring at his lap. "I think some of that weight I've been carrying will soon be lifted."

She gave his shoulders one more squeeze before clasping her hands in front of her. "You don't know how delighted I am to hear that. Now, the business question, are you playing piano for us tomorrow night?"

He looked up at her and smiled. "I wouldn't miss it for the world."

"Good—and are you staying for the ceilidh later in the evening?"

"I don't know…I've never been to one."

Her mouth fell open in shock. "You've been in our lovely country for a year and you haven't yet been to a ceilidh?" Before he could answer, she said, "Well, you're staying for it tomorrow night. You can bring that Grant fellow."

Before he could politely decline, she stood and returned to the bar.

Friday, 1:42 AM

That same crappy pop song played out on the radio's small speakers. Try as he might, Jake couldn't continue denying his growing love for it. He bobbed his head while wiping down the kitchen counters and pulling out the big metal bowl for the scones.

Jake yawned, exhausted. The day had been long and draining. The torrent of emotions slamming into him all day had ebbed, but in its place was regret…regret for telling off his dad a couple days ago. He felt like an ass now that the whole story was out. But, Jake kept reminding himself, he hadn't known the full story back then, so he shouldn't beat himself down for that. And if he hadn't had that outburst, the full story might never have come out. The outburst seemed to have set in motion a much closer relationship with his parents, his dad especially. So, maybe it was a good thing?

"Are you Jake?"

He spun around, unaware that anyone had come in. A gangly, young twink with thick-rimmed glasses stood there in a pair of shorts and a brown T-shirt. The front of his shorts tented with a bulge.

This was not the day to get into this.

"I am. Can I help you with anything?" Jake kept all seductiveness from his voice and turned back to his task. He opened the cupboard and pulled out the box of scone mix.

"I, uh, heard that…well, are you…I need, uh…" The twink's voice wavered.

Jake closed his eyes and hung his head. He wasn't in the mood for a blowjob, but he couldn't keep torturing this young man, expecting him to eventually work up the courage to ask and then be shot down. He turned around, crossed his arms, and leaned against the counter.

"Yeah, I'm Jake. And, yeah, I'm the guy you probably heard about. I give blowjobs. But today's not a good day and I don't think tomorrow or the next day will be good, either. I'm sorry."

The twink's cheeks flushed a dark red and his eyes avoided Jake's.

"Yeah, whatever," he muttered. The twink walked out, the door quietly swinging closed behind him.

Jake turned back to the bowl. As he reached to put away the box of mix, the door opened again behind him. *Fucking wankers.* He shook his head and turned around, then caught his breath.

"Hi."

"Hi." Grant had on a loose pair of boxers and a wrinkled, red shirt. His face still had that delightful scruff. It looked good on him.

Jake watched him, unsure what this visit was about, unsure what he wanted to say.

"I couldn't find you all day," Grant said, stepping forward and leaning a hip against the island.

"I didn't really want to be found." Jake stepped toward the island and leaned forward, resting his elbows on the cold, hard surface.

"Still moving to Croatia?"

Jake examined the man's eyes, seeking intent. His brown orbs were warm and caring, calm and patient. "Would you like a pot of tea?"

A smile touched Grant's lips. "I would love a pot of tea."

"So what did you get up to today?" Jake pulled out the kettle and set it on the stove, pulled out the teapot and put in a bag of peppermint, and then grabbed two mugs.

"Oh, the usual, you know. I took in some scenery, went for a run, walked across the bridge to pick up a few groceries." He leaned forward on the island, watching

Jake. "I'm planning a drive through the countryside tomorrow."

"Oh, yeah?"

"It's been a long while since I've just explored Skye. There's so much beauty out there, just a short jaunt away. It would be a shame to be so close and not take it in."

Jake poured the boiling water into the teapot, then picked it up, along with the mugs. "Let's go into the common room." Grant followed him as they walked through the darkness. Familiar with the layout of the building with no light, Jake set the tea on a side table and switched on a dim lamp between two well-worn chairs.

Grant sat in one chair and waited until Jake sat in the other before asking the question Jake knew he had been dying to ask. "So…why didn't you want to be found today?"

Jake leaned back in his chair and struggled with how to begin. "I finally returned my mom's calls. As soon as she popped up on the screen, my dad sat down next to her."

"Oh…" Grant poured their tea and handed a mug to Jake. "So you're moving further away than Croatia? Japan?"

"No…I'm not sure what I'm going to do." Jake took a sip of his tea, letting his mind wander a bit. "I was wrong about my dad. Totally wrong."

"Hmm. I noticed you used to call him 'father', now it's 'dad'."

"When my dad was in school, his best friend was a boy named Jake." From there, the rest of the story tumbled out of him.

"Wow. Talk about a one-eighty—from thinking he doesn't like you to knowing he loves you. You are a very lucky man, Jake." Grant set his empty mug on the table. "I don't understand why you're not rushing back to Canada to be with your family."

Jake stared into his empty mug, quashing thoughts of Peter. "It's a little more complicated than that." Thankfully, Grant didn't pursue.

"Tomorrow's your night off, right?"

Jake smiled. "Yeah. I'm going to play some piano at the pub late into the evening and then maybe hang around for the ceilidh."

Grant raised an eyebrow. "You don't strike me as the ceilidh type."

"Perhaps not. I must confess I've never been."

"You've been in Scotland for *a year* and not only have you not toured Skye, but you've not been to a ceilidh? Just what have you done with yourself for a year?"

"Well," Jake chuckled. "You know some of what I've been doing."

Grant rolled his eyes. "Back when I first arrived, we made plans for Friday. Given all that's happened since then, I'd assumed they were off. Tell you what—let's put those plans back on—be my date tomorrow. We'll drive out through Skye and have a picnic, then come back for you to play piano at the pub, and we'll dance the night away at the ceilidh."

Try as he might, Jake couldn't fight the internal flutter of anxiety at the word "date". He swallowed, forcing that anxiety down. "Sounds like a nice day."

Grant narrowed his eyes. "Date. You can say the word. Date."

Jake swallowed again. "Sounds like a nice date."

Grant put a hand on Jake's knee. "Don't sound so terrified. Look at it this way—it's a date with no risk of commitment. I'll be going back to Edinburgh soon and you'll be, I don't know, moving off to somewhere, probably. It's like a hookup, but a date. It's a date-up."

"All right, I think I can do a date-up."

"In that case, I'm going to get some rest. We'll head out as soon as you're up—so don't sleep in too late." Grant stood and, before Jake could avoid it, he planted a quick kiss on Jake's forehead, then darted out of the room and up the stairs.

Chapter Thirteen

Friday, 1:07 PM

"YOU'RE UP EARLY." AUDRA GREETED Jake as soon as he was in sight of the front desk.

"I've got a field trip today."

Audra paused her video. "You mean 'date', don't you?" She leaned on her elbows and made dreamy eyes at him. "Our little Jake has a date."

"You've been talking to Grant."

"He wanted to know what foods you like for your picnic." She batted innocent eyelashes at him again. "Are you two going to snog all day?"

"It's not a date, by the way."

A firm hand clapped down on his shoulder and gripped there. Jake glanced over his shoulder to find Grant smiling at him. "Oh, it's a date, all right. And there *will* be snogging."

"I need breakfast first." As Jake turned to walk away, leaving the two gossipers to carry on, Grant's hand slid around, wrapping his arm around Jake's shoulders. His embrace was warm.

"I saved a couple of your scones for you, and I've got the kettle heating to make you a fresh mug of tea to go." He squeezed again. "You wait here and I'll go finish up your tea."

Grant walked back toward the kitchen, allowing Jake to take in the view from behind. Grant wore full Scottish regalia today, with the kilt curving around his perfect ass and showcasing his delightfully hairy legs.

"Mmm," Audra said. "He looks delicious."

"That he does."

Friday, 2:15 PM

Jake brushed the last few scone crumbs off his legs and onto the floor of Grant's compact, but comfortable rental car. He took the final swig of still-warm tea from the insulated mug and put it back in the cup holder. The endless country and overcast skies, rather dull and dreary, stretched out around them as far as Jake could see. The only living things in sight were a smattering of sheep and a few cattle roaming through the hills.

"I'm glad you could come today," Grant said.

"Me too. I think I needed some time away from it all." He hoped sunglasses hid the fact that he kept staring at Grant's thighs. The kilt had ridden up quite a bit. Jake had to stop looking, otherwise his half-stiff dick would be rock hard and very noticeable. He forced himself to look out at the endlessly boring landscape.

"So how are you? You've had quite a week."

"I'm okay, I guess. I think I'm back to where I was at the beginning of the week. Do I stay here longer or go home?"

"No more Croatia?"

"No more Croatia."

After a long silence, Grant said, "You could visit Edinburgh. Visit me."

Grant appeared hopeful and sheepish, lacking the confidence that he always seemed to project. "Maybe. It's complicated."

"So you keep saying," Grant said. Jake tried to pull hidden meanings out of that, but couldn't find anything.

Above them, the clouds parted slightly, bringing some brightness and warmth. Grant slowed the car as they approached a flock of sheep gathered on the road.

"I think we'll stop here."

"Here?" Jake turned his head around in both directions. "There's nothing here. Can't you just go around the sheep?"

"In this car? No, off-roading isn't an option." Grant turned off the engine. As the noise of the motor cut off, the sound of bleating sheep surrounded them. "Besides, this might be nature's way of telling us this is our picnic spot—the sun came out and the road, for us, ends here.

We pretty much made it as far as I'd been hoping to, anyway."

Jake searched in all directions. "I am totally confused. We're in the middle of nowhere. How can this be where you want to go? We passed through Portree a half hour ago—that was at least a city, this is a field!"

Grant winked at him and got out of the car. He pulled his backpack out of the back seat. Hurriedly, Jake followed suit, grabbing his own backpack.

"When you're looking around, do you actually *see* what's in front of you?" Grant waved his hand out in front of him. "Look at the hills."

Jake acquiesced and took in his surroundings. He knit his brow. "Weird. All the hills are tiny and they're, like, rippled."

"Welcome to Faerie Glen." He grabbed Jake's hand and led him through the sheep, who largely scattered as they approached. "It's a place of magic and wonder."

Before Jake could pull his hand back, Grant intertwined his fingers with Jake's. He decided to let Grant keep doing this; it felt comfortable. New, but comfortable.

"We're going on a hike to Castle Ewen." They walked across the field until they reached a well-worn footpath that meandered through the hills. Grant let go of Jake's hand as they walked single-file along the dirt path.

Jake examined the hills as they passed. He'd never thought he'd be so captivated by scenery. There were no bars, no clubs, no internet, no bathhouse…yet this was where he wanted to be. Sheep and highland cattle, with long hair dangling in their eyes, dotted the landscape.

Grant led them up to the top of one of the rippled hills. "See that rock formation over there? That's Castle Ewen."

"So it's not really a castle?"

"No, just a large rock that juts up into the sky. Families usually hike out here and the kids climb the castle." He reached out and squeezed Jake's hand again. "We're going to picnic on top of it."

Five minutes later they were scaling Castle Ewen. The rock formation had plenty of handholds and footholds. With Grant leading the way, Jake had a good view from behind and below. His cock grew hard in his pants as he watched that ass sway above his head.

From the top of Castle Ewen, Jake could see the entire bumpy landscape of Faerie Glen, the hills and ripples creating a majestic sight. As Jake stood at the edge of the rock and looked out over the glen, Grant unzipped his backpack and set up the picnic.

"It's beautiful," Jake said, barely above a whisper.

"It is, isn't it?" Grant wrapped his arms around Jake from behind, pressing his crotch into Jake's ass. "I couldn't think of a better way to experience Faerie Glen than with you."

Jake felt his old anxiety bubbling up the longer Grant had his arms wrapped around him. He felt constricted, suffocated. "I'm hungry," Jake said, pulling them apart before the anxiety became a problem.

If Grant picked up on it, he didn't make an issue of it. "Good. I brought some sandwiches, iced tea, and cookies." He turned Jake around and swept his arm out, as if presenting a display. A soft blue blanket lay across the grass and rock, with their lunch placed in the middle.

As they ate, they chatted idly about nothing of importance. Jake preferred it that way right now. He wasn't ready to get into serious discussion about home.

"Now what?" Jake put the lid back on the cookie container and ran a napkin across his mouth.

"Now...now we relax. Skye is not an island to be rushed—it's an island to be absorbed and experienced." He stood up and walked toward the edge, motioning for Jake to join him.

Jake got to his feet and walked over. The view, now that he was settling into this new appreciation of rural Scotland, was breathtaking. Grant wrapped his hand around Jake's waist, resting on the top of his ass. He knew what Grant wanted and finally felt ready to give it to him, give him something he'd only given one other man before. He wrapped his arm around Grant's waist and pulled him in close. Closing his eyes, Jake puckered his lips, and leaned forward.

His mouth touched Grant's, spreading a tingling warmth, radiating from that point of contact. Jake's heart skipped a couple beats as he gave in, allowing his feelings to lead without his head interfering. It had been a long time since he'd kissed—he remember the last time with perfect clarity—but the movements felt natural, coming back to him without effort.

His tongue pressed out and against Grant's lips, gently parting them and brushing against the man's teeth and tongue. Jake brought a hand up to Grant's face, running it over the sexy stubble the man had decided to keep today. He slid his other hand down Grant's ass and grabbed a handful of the thick bubble butt.

Grant moaned and returned the grope with a squeeze of Jake's ass. He pulled Jake tighter, crushing their chests together, grinding their cocks together.

They stumbled back to the blanket and Jake tore off Grant's coat and opened his shirt. His chest was well-formed and hairy in all the right places. The nipples were hard, poking through the short hair. Jake ran his fingers over Grant's chest and nipped and licked at his nipples.

Grant groaned and ran his hands through Jake's hair, massaging his scalp. He suddenly rolled them over so that Grant was on top, then lifted Jake's shirt to get to his smooth chest. His tongue licked a trail from one of Jake's nipples to the other, and then down to his navel. Jake giggled and kicked as Grant's tongue probed his belly button.

Jake sat up and shucked off his shirt. He pulled Grant in for another passionate kiss and ran his hands along Grant's kilted hips. He gripped the Scot and rolled them over again, so Jake was again the dominating one. His heart beat rapidly as he reached to do the action he'd been dreaming about all week. Jake grasped the bottom hem of Grant's kilt and lifted it up. *Damn! There goes the no-underwear fantasy!*

Grant wore a pair of tight-fitting red briefs, with a large bulge and a prominent wet spot. His dick was about six or seven inches long and just the right thickness, perfect proportions that made it a delight to play with. Jake fondled it, brought his face close enough to smell it, to inhale the scent of man and sweat and lust. Then he dragged his tongue across the length of the bulge, while his hand fondled Grant's balls and teased his taint.

"Do it." Grant's words were a harsh whisper, filled with need. "Suck me."

Jake pulled off the man's briefs and did what he did best. He took Grant's cock head in his mouth and swirled his tongue around it. The slit was sweet and salty with the taste of precum, tastier than he'd had in a long time.

He gripped the base and slid his mouth down the entire length of Grant's cock until the tip brushed against the back of his throat. Jake couldn't get into the mechanical motions with Grant. This was too important, this was too intimate to get him off mechanically. Jake massaged Grant's dick with his tongue and he slowly slid up and down, stimulating Grant's every nerve ending with pressure and suction and moisture and warmth.

Grant's gasps and moans echoed through Faerie Glen and his hands gripped Jake's head in a passionate embrace. Grant's hips bucked with each mouthful of cock Jake took in.

Jake pulled Grant's dick out of his mouth and jacked him with a fist. He shoved his fingers in his mouth, making them wet and slippery, then ran those fingers over Grant's tight hole. It puckered beneath his touch. He forced a finger in to the first knuckle. When it was loose and comfortable, Jake pushed a second finger in.

"Oh, fuck!" Grant bucked wildly.

With one hand digging into Grant's ass and the other stroking his cock, Jake sucked the man's balls into his mouth. He licked and tugged, pulled and massaged.

"Oh, God," Grant gasped. "I can't take it anymore. Fuck me, Jake. Fuck me. Drive it in hard."

Jake's already hard cock solidified even more. He ached for release, with a deep need he hadn't felt for a long time. He quickly yanked off his jeans and briefs.

From his position on his back, Grant reached to his backpack and pulled out a condom and a small packet of lube.

Jake opened the lube and squirted a dab on his fingers, then rubbed it against Grant's tight hole. He worked his fingers in and out, relaxing and widening his ass. When he could fit three fingers in, without too much of a wince from Grant, Jake rolled the condom on and spread the rest of the lube on top.

Grant pulled his legs back, holding them under the knees, and Jake slid in close, fitting his body in with Grant's. Jake pressed the head of his cock against Grant's rosebud. Slowly, it gave way, expanding, eagerly consuming Jake's dick. Jake went in, inch by inch, until he was buried to the hilt between Grant's furry cheeks.

"That feels so good. So warm and tight." Jake's eyes fell closed. He hadn't topped in more than a year; he'd almost forgotten what it was like. Beneath him, Grant was almost breathless with ecstasy.

Jake dragged his cock out until just the head was in Grant, then slid it back in to the hilt. He rocked back and forth, picking up speed and varying his momentum, always going deep. Sweat beaded on his forehead and back, rolling down his body and dripping on to Grant, mingling with the Scot's own sweat. Beneath him, Grant gripped his hand around his cock and pumped in time with Jake's thrusts.

"Oh, fuck, I'm close! I'm gonna blow soon."

"Do it," Grant urged. "Fill me."

As the tingle of pleasure and orgasm rose, Jake pumped harder, slamming his cock into Grant's ass with passion and force. Grant grunted with each thrust, his fist still keeping time. Grant's face contorted with pleasure and he moaned as orgasm overcame him and he shot hot, white cum all over his chest, mixing with the beaded sweat.

Grant's sphincter tightened sharply with his orgasm, pressuring Jake's cock and sending him over the edge of orgasm. He drove his dick in deeper, as deep as it would go, pressed tightly against Grant's body, as heat rocketed out of him and filled the condom.

Jake gasped and collapsed on top of Grant, his cock sliding out of the man's ass. Grant held him tight, kissing him along his jaw.

Somewhere below them, a sheep bleated.

Chapter Fourteen

Friday, 7:55 PM

JAKE'S FINGERS MOVED RAPIDLY FROM KEY to key, pounding out a jaunty folk tune. The heat of Grant's body, sitting next to him, reminded him of only hours earlier when they were naked, sweaty, and in each other's cum-covered embrace. Jake stumbled over a string of notes, his mind elsewhere, but recovered before anyone was likely to notice.

The pub was filled with patrons, about half from the hostel and half from the townsfolk. It was hot and sweaty and loud. As the tune came to an end and Jake pounded out the flourish, a smattering of applause chased through the crowd. He never got much applause, but knew his music was creating atmosphere, not standing out as performance.

He reached for the beer glass Grant had placed on top of the piano and took a swig.

Grant's arm snaked around his waist. "You're really good!"

Jake smiled, but glanced around to see if anyone noticed their closeness. "Thanks."

Grant seemed to take the hint and took his arm back. He didn't seem too hurt. "I ordered you a burger and chips. They should be here soon."

As if in response, Jake's stomach grumbled, loud enough for Grant to notice through the pub's clamor. He smiled and winked. "We worked up quite an appetite earlier today."

Jake glanced around to ensure no one was nearby, then leaned in to whisper into Grant's ear. "Thanks for being patient with me. Today was really special. It's been a long time since someone treated me so well and made me feel so good." Jake was still buzzing from the emotional high he had reached.

Grant leaned in to whisper back, his breath hot and moist on Jake's ear, stirring his cock. "Like I kept telling you, you deserve all that—you just needed to let yourself accept it."

"Thanks, Grant." Jake took another swallow of beer and then bounced into another folk tune. He had worked from a book when first playing at the pub, but the tunes quickly became familiar. His fingers moved with muscle memory, creating a melody that had Grant bouncing his knee in time.

Halfway through the song, their food came. Grant fed Jake chips as he played on. When the song was over, Jake devoured half his food. He then played one last tune before shutting the lid on the piano keys. Another smattering of applause resounded through the room, louder than earlier.

Grant grabbed their plates and Jake carried their beers and his backpack as they headed to an empty table in the corner of the pub. "Have you thought more about what you want to do when your year is up?"

"No. It's too much right now."

"Because I was serious about what I said before. If you want to stay another year but move to Edinburgh, you could stay with me." Grant's voice was unsteady, lacking the rock-solid confidence it usually carried.

Jake hesitated before responding. He didn't want to hurt Grant. "Thanks for the offer. I'm still totally lost. I need to think it through. And there's always the chance they won't renew my work visa and this is all moot anyway."

Grant's face fell a little before he reinforced it with a smile. "Okay, cool. I just wanted to make sure you had the option."

The sound of a bow sliding across a fiddle cut through the noise. The ceilidh band was in the process of setting up and tuning.

"And you said you've *never* been to a ceilidh?" Grant's face showed mock shock.

"No, I just never hung around this long—at this point, I'd usually go for a walk or to watch the stars from the ruins." Jake wiped his fingers on the napkin. The band jumped into a lively number. "I'm still not too sure if I want to stick around. I'm not much of a dancer."

Grant waved his hand dismissively. "I can't dance, either, but I can enjoy a ceilidh just fine. You just follow along and have fun!"

Jake watched as the crowd assembled themselves into two lines, facing each other. They were roughly split along gender, but there was a mixture in each line. Before he could watch the dance unfold from a safe distance, Grant grabbed his hand and pulled him to the lines, facing him. Jake's eyes widened and his heart thumped with fear, but he held back from bolting. The afternoon had been amazing because he'd opened up and trusted. This evening could bring the same.

Suddenly the pair at the end grabbed each other and dance down the aisle. The lines of people moved and contorted with the ease of practice. Faces were filled with laughter and smiles and no one cared that Jake was awkwardly half a step behind and his forehead was covered in cold sweat. Far too soon, Jake found himself at the head of the line with Grant. The Scot took the lead and grabbed Jake, bouncing down the line with him.

As they stumbled toward the end of their movements, Jake laughed and Grant gave him a hug, then they separated and returned to their lines. Jake gave into the music. It was like playing the piano—he had to stop thinking and let the rhythm move him, let the notes lead him.

With a few more beers and a lot more dancing, Jake and Grant stumbled out of the pub well after midnight. They stopped to steady each other, hugging tight. The scent of Grant wafted up to Jake's nostrils, causing his breath to catch and his cock to harden.

"Let's go to the castle," Jake said with urgency. He slung his backpack over his shoulder and grabbed Grant's hand, pulling him toward the edge of town and up the hill to the ruins of Dunakin Castle. He stumbled on a tangle of roots and fell to the ground, his backpack falling beside him, Grant tumbling on top of him. Grant's rock-hard dick ground into his ass, sending a new jolt of lust to his own cock.

"Fuck, I want you so bad." Grant covered the back of Jake's neck with kisses.

Jake rolled over so his chest pressed against Grant's. "Not here. Too visible. Up in the ruins." He pushed Grant off and breathlessly got back on his feet, grabbed his backpack, and scrambled up the hill. When Grant came bumping into him, Jake grabbed the man and pushed him against the remains of a wall, holding him tight against the ancient stone. He crushed his lips against Grant's, forcing his tongue into his mouth. Grant moaned and sagged against the stone.

Grant's hands found their way under Jake's shirt and pulled it over his head. The cool night air brushed against Jake's nipples, making them hard as his cock. He fumbled with the buttons on Grant's shirt, revealing that hairy chest just one step at a time. With the shirt open, Jake abandoned Grant's lips and sucked on his nipples, abrading his teeth against them just enough to make Grant's knees shake.

Jake felt Grant's hands at his belt, yanking the buckle and tearing his jeans open. Jake shoved his pants and briefs down, stepping out of them and his shoes at the same time. As he moved up to kissing and tonguing Grant's neck, his hands wandered around the top of Grant's kilt, searching for a clasp or button. After torturous long moments of fumbling, Grant's hands moved along the kilt's waist and it instantly fell to the ground.

Fuck, yeah. No underwear. Jake grasped Grant's hard, thick, and leaking cock, his hand instantly wet and slippery with precum. He stroked with one hand and pinched Grant's nipples with the other, kissing him passionately. Grant's hands found their way to Jake's cock and balls, one hand on each, tugging. Grant pulled him close and pressed their dicks together, grasping them both in one large hand, stroking up and down.

"Can I fuck you?" Grant asked.

Jake stopped kissing, frozen in instant fear. His heart beat so hard, threatening to burst out of his ribs. His mind ran through all of the possible pain, stirring up his age-old anxiety. He bit his lip, forcing his anxiety down. *Following only my emotions this afternoon led to heaven. I can do it again.*

"Yes, but be gentle." Jake couldn't keep the quiver out of his voice.

"Trust me. I'll treat you right. I'll rim you and get you nice and loose and wet, and then I'll go in slow and smooth." He kissed along Jake's jaw, ending at his ear. "I want you, Jake."

Follow my emotions, not my brain.

"Okay."

Grant kissed him, his tongue exploring Jake's mouth, then pulled back. "Get down, face down. I want to pleasure that gorgeous ass of yours."

Trust him, trust him, trust him...

Jake got down on his hands and knees on the soft earth. Behind him, Grant shifted, then a world of warm and wet pleasure shot through him. Grant's tongue and lips circled around Jake's hole, gently probed it, then returned to circling. With a groan, Jake's arms gave out and he rested the side of his face on the grass, his ass sticking high in the air. Grant put a hand on each ass cheek and spread them wide, digging his tongue in deeper with more force.

The pleasure radiating from Jake's ass overwhelmed everything else. All he was, was a being of pleasure, all originating from his hole.

When he thought his ass couldn't stretch anymore and he couldn't take much more, Grant pressed a finger in deep, brushing Jake's prostate, sending a thick drop of precum out of his quivering cock. The one finger was soon joined by a second, sliding in and out. Grant moistened his hole with saliva again, making the fingers slicker, spreading Jake's ass wider.

"Are you ready?"

Jake nodded, face rubbing against the ground. Realizing it was dark and Grant wouldn't be able to see his nod, Jake said, "God, yes."

"Hang on." Grant zipped open Jake's backpack and a couple minutes later, as soon as Jake caught his breath, the hard, wide head of Grant's cock was pressing into Jake's tight hole.

Jake grunted. The pain was intense.

"Jack off, take your mind off it."

Jake reached under himself and grabbed hold of his cock and stroked furiously. In his ass, it was like something gave way and all of a sudden Grant slid in smoothly to the hilt. His pelvis pressed warmly and firmly against Jake's ass, an erotic contrast to the cool night air on the rest of his skin.

As Grant slid his cock slowly out of Jake's ass, Jake was again overcome by sensation. He let out his breath in a long, raspy groan and his hand fell from his dick, unable to concentrate enough to beat off. Grant pushed in again and the head of his cock must have pressed against Jake's prostate because in a flash his world of pleasure became immensely more intense. Jake's cock quivered again and leaked a steady stream, falling to the ground beneath him.

When Grant pulled out and back in again, another surge of ecstasy raced from Jake's prostate to his cock. Each hit brought the intensity higher, the climax closer. Grant gripped his hands tightly on Jake's hips, holding him steady. Jake whimpered with every thrust, unable to think, to respond, to jack off.

Suddenly, another hit on Jake's prostate sent his pleasure hurtling over a cliff. Hot cum shot out of Jake's cock, striking his chest and painting the ground beneath him. His shout of release echoed among the stone.

Grant pumped harder, slamming into Jake's ass. Moments later, the fingers on Jake's hips gripped tighter, digging into his flesh. Grant let out a strangled sound and his body tensed, then he collapsed on top of Jake, kissing his moist back.

Chapter Fifteen

Saturday, 1:37 AM

FUCK, FUCK, FUCK, FUCK, FUCK, FUCK, fuck." Jake paced back and forth in the common area, trying to keep his swears to a whisper. When his pacing brought him back to the chair, he rifled through all the pockets of his backpack again, digging and searching. "Fucking hell."

From somewhere behind him, the delicious smell of baking biscuits wafted through the air, under the care of the other night staff. Absently, Jake wondered what sort of trouble Andrew got into at this hour of the night. There was no way he was squeaky clean. *Does he give blowjobs too?* Jake wondered.

The click of the door snapped his attention back. Grant came in, flashlight in hand.

"Did you find it?" Jake demanded, pleading.

Grant smiled and held up his other hand, holding Jake's leather-bound notebook. It must have fallen out of his backpack in the rush for condoms at Dunakin Castle. Jake took it, relieved to see and hold it again, and suddenly felt the need to hug it tight. If he had lost it earlier in the day, at Faerie Glen, he would never have seen it again.

"Thank you, Grant. This really means a lot to me."

He smiled, but there was something off. "You're welcome, Jake. I'm glad I was able to find it."

Jake picked up his backpack and slung it over his shoulder. He gave Grant a quick kiss on the cheek. "Thanks for the amazing date. I had a wonderful time."

"Me, too." He kissed Jake's forehead and rubbed his hands on Jake's arms. "Jake…who's Peter?"

Jake felt like the floor gave way under him. "Huh? What?"

"Peter." He pointed at the notebook in Jake's tight grip. "When I found that, I flipped through it to make sure it was yours. I saw the note in the front…and the letters."

Jake felt his cheeks warm with a flush. In his panic, it hadn't occurred to him that Grant might see the words inside. He knew the dedication well, scrawled in Peter's messy handwriting.

> *Dear Jake,*
> *I hope this notebook provides a place to record your memories, write out your dreams, document your*

experiences, and provide you with a link to home.
Remember that I will be right here, waiting for your
return, eager to share in your year of adventure
through stories and laughter.
    Love, Peter

He felt his mouth quiver and his eyes water. He didn't want this discussion. Not now.

Grant tenderly put a hand on Jake's arm. "You've let me in to your world today, Jake. We shared so much together. Please, tell me about Peter."

When Jake didn't say no, Grant led him back to the comfortable chairs on either side of the weak lamp. "So...Peter...?"

"Peter...Peter is my friend back home." Jake took a steadying breath. "Well, maybe more than a friend. He's gay, too. We met in our first year of university and became really good friends. It didn't take long before we started...started fucking." Jake searched for judgment in Grant's face, but found none. "We settled into a friends-with-benefits situation. We'd fuck and suck regularly, but there was no romance, just friendship."

"I'm guessing things didn't stay that way."

Jake shook his head. "It didn't take long for Peter to develop stronger feelings for me. He tried to hide them at first, but eventually he told me, though I had sort of picked up on them already. I...I think I had the same feelings for him, but was too scared to admit it. I lied and told him that I wanted us to just be friends. But it was obvious when we…when we made love. You'd asked if I'd ever kissed a man or loved a man. The answer to both is yes, and it's Peter."

"Hmm." Grant leaned back, the chair groaning with the shift in weight. "Do you think this ties into what you've said about your dad?"

Jake's eyes watered more and he swiped at them. "Maybe. Probably." He exhaled a shuddered breath. "Yeah. The only message I got, or what I thought I was getting, was that gay was wrong. I thought my dad would only accept it to a certain point and I sort of accepted that limitation, I think. I loved Peter, but was terrified of the consequences."

Grant reached over and settled his hand on top of Jake's. The warmth and weight of it provided some grounding, some foundation.

"I think Peter knew I was lying about my feelings. He backed off a bit, returning us to friends-with-benefits, but he started leaving some stuff in my locker at university, claiming some of my space as shared space with him. And we still kissed…a lot. But when we graduated, it suddenly became too much. I couldn't segment my life so much anymore—Peter's stuff that was in my locker moved to my bedroom. He had claimed space in my home, the same home I shared with my parents."

Grant's fingers wrapped around Jake's and squeezed. "Then you came here."

"Then I came here. I felt suffocated and needed to escape. I thought running away from home would mean running away from my problems."

"That didn't work, did it?"

"No." Jake shook his head and looked down at his knees. "If anything, the distance and separation has made it clear to me that I need...that I still love Peter."

Grant's grip on Jake's hand loosened considerably. Jake felt an invisible wall erect between them.

"And your conversation with your father...it removed some of the suffocation...didn't it?"

"Yes." Jake's voice had grown meek and quiet. "I'm sorry if I led you on."

For a long stretch of heartbeats, Jake didn't know what to expect. Would Grant get angry or say it's okay? Would he just get up and walk away?

Grant sighed and visibly collected himself. "We both knew this was just for the day, that it wasn't going anywhere."

"You wanted me to move in with you in Edinburgh." Jake still stared at his knees.

"I did, didn't I? I got caught up in our date. I saw you hurting, I felt a need to take care of you...and we work so well together. And it doesn't hurt that you're damn cute." Suddenly, Grant's fingers wrapped around Jake's again, bringing back the warmth and closeness. "I saw how special you are and wanted to keep you, even though I knew I wouldn't be able to. We're different people, Jake, and we come from different lives. We intersected for one glorious day in one of the most magical places on Earth."

"I really enjoyed our date." He finally looked back up at Grant. His face expressed a mixture of happiness and wistfulness. "You helped me. So much. You opened up my heart and made it possible for me to risk being hurt for the reward of joy."

Grant stood and pulled Jake to his feet. He wrapped his arms around Jake and pulled him in to a tight and loving hug. "I will never forget you, Jake. And I will never be mad at you because your heart belongs to someone else. If anything, I want you to be as happy as you can be, and I see that Peter is the man that does that to you." Grant kissed Jake on the cheek. "Don't let Peter slip through your fingers. I can tell you love him. He is one very lucky man."

"Thank you."

Chapter Sixteen

THE STAFF DORM IN THE ATTIC WAS mercifully empty. Jake closed the door and sat on his bed, flipping open his laptop. His heart raced and his palms were clammy. Opening the chat program, he was both happy and terrified to find Peter's icon showed him as online.

Acting before fear could paralyze him, and with memories of Grant's words urging him on, he double-clicked Peter's icon to open a video chat with him. Seconds later, Peter accepted and the man that always made him horny filled his screen.

"Jake? It's been so long! How are you?"

"Hi, Peter." *Damn, he's cute.* "I'm…I'm good. How are you?"

He smiled, showing perfect teeth. "I was having a good morning, but it's much better now that I'm talking to you." Peter winked at him.

Jake didn't know if he needed to explain, but felt compelled to. "I'm sorry for being so quiet for so long. I've just, I don't know, gotten caught up in life around here."

"Must be an exciting place. I looked it up online— Kyleakin, eh? Can't get much wilder than that…what with it's sleepy approach to life."

Jake chuckled. He loved Peter's dry humor. But, still, there was uneasiness in the pit of his stomach. Now that he had Peter on the screen, he didn't know what to say…how to start.

When the silence lapsed for far too long, Peter prodded him. "So, if you're calling me after ten months of not, it must be something important." He brushed a bit of hair behind his ear.

"Yeah," Jake said. He steeled himself and opened his mouth. "I haven't been fair to you for a very long time. And I've come to realize that me moving to Scotland for a year was me more or less running from the situation. I wasn't ready to face it and I feel I've wronged you."

Peter lost his smile. "I agree." He leaned closer to the screen and his smile made a brief reappearance. "I know you've had your issues, mostly with your father, and I understand. I can't say I'm okay with it, but I do understand. Not everyone's journey is easy."

His dad's conversation replayed in the back of his mind. "Remind me later to tell you a story. My dad and I are better than we've been in years." Before Peter could ask about it and take the call down that road, Jake continued, "I think it's time we had a talk about you and me."

"Oh, yeah?" Peter looked as if he was preparing for a letdown.

"You know I love you, and you've probably known it for far longer than I have."

Peter grinned and leaned in close, as if secretly whispering to Jake. "When you look at me, you've got this glimmer in your eyes. I can even see it now, across these thousands of miles and through the webcam. You look at me the way no one else ever looks at me."

Jake suddenly felt self-conscious and looked down at his hands, but forced his gaze back up to the screen. "These ten months in Scotland...well, they weren't necessarily a mistake. I've grown a lot—mostly in the last week—and I've learned a lot about myself. What I've learned is that if you love someone, you have to take that chance. You have to take that risk and go for it. Because if you don't, if you miss your chance, you never know if it'll ever come around again. And what I've discovered is that I've denied my heart for too long. I hope, I really hope, that you will give me a second chance. Peter, will you go out with me?"

"Well," Peter said, still looking serious. "I don't know..."

Jake couldn't tell if Peter was serious if this was more of his dry humor. "Please, let me make it up to you."

"Hmm…" Try as he might, Peter couldn't hold back a broad grin. "Of course, I'll go out with you! When's our date? Do I need to fly to Scotland for you to take me out for coffee? I'll have to see if I can hitch a ride."

Jake's smile matched Peter's. His heart thudded with excitement and the sourness was gone from his stomach. He'd faced the hardest part and gotten through it.

"By the way," Peter said, "since *you* asked *me*, you get to pay for our date."

Jake stuck out his tongue. "You're kind of worth it, so I'm okay with that."

"*Kind of* worth it? Well!" Peter pretended to flip his hair. "In that case, you can take me on an expensive date."

Jake laughed. "Oh, Peter, I've missed you. I've missed you so much."

Peter leaned in close to the screen. "And I've missed you. Come home, Jake."

"I will. Soon. I'll be racing home."

"I love you, Jake."

"And I love you, Peter, so much." He laughed. "God, it feels good to say that out loud. I love you, Peter."

A few minutes later of idle chatter and plans for Jake's return, Jake shut his computer and hurried down the stairs to find Grant.

"So?" Grant knew Jake's plan, helped him figure out the words to say.

"He said yes!"

Grant beamed with joy. "Oh, I'm so happy for you, Jake!" He pulled him into another hug and planted a kiss on his forehead. "I'm so happy for you."

Epilogue

One month later

JAKE STOOD ON THE FRONT STEP OF Peter's apartment building.

His heart thudded in his chest, constricting his throat. He'd come home to Canada last night and his parents had picked him up from the airport. His mom had hugged him so tight and made him promise to stay in Canada. Knowing that Peter was here in Canada, it wasn't hard to reassure his mom that he wasn't going anywhere soon.

Today, though, was the big day.

He'd spent an hour in front of the mirror in his room, trying to get just the right outfit. He knew he didn't really have to impress Peter, that they'd already won each other's hearts, but it didn't feel right to not put effort into it.

He typed in Peter's code.

"Jake?" The intercom added a heavy crackle of static to Peter's voice.

"Yup." His heart thudded even harder.

Peter buzzed him in and he almost vaulted up the stairs to the next floor, then hurried down the hallway. As soon as he reached the door, it opened.

"Peter," Jake said, saying his name like a prayer.

"Come in," Peter said. He stepped back and swept his hand out, inviting Jake in.

He came in, looked around, but inevitably found his gaze drawn to Peter. Beside them, the door slowly swung shut and clicked as it closed. *Have you ever kissed a man?* Grant's words rung in his head again.

He put a hand on Peter's chest and another at the back of his head and pulled Peter in, crashing his lips against Peter's, kissing him with a year's worth of pent-up emotions and lust and need. Peter kissed back, pushing his tongue into Jake's mouth. Jake moved his hands, wrapped his arms around Peter, and pulled him even closer. He could feel his lover's hard cock mash against his.

Without a word spoken between them, and without breaking their kiss longer than a second or two, they stumbled into Peter's bedroom and tore each other's clothes off. Jake finally broke the kiss to look down at Peter's body, splayed out beneath him. He was still as trim and fit as before, a piece of art, a work of beauty. *And he's mine.* But it was more than just the physical that had attracted him to Peter—it was the mind, the personality, the *human being*.

He bent down and kissed Peter's neck, trailing hot kisses down his chest and his stomach, finally stopping at Peter's cock. Then he took him in his mouth, sucking on that dick he'd sucked on so many times before.

But it was different now. This time, there was love. It wasn't just lust. And it wasn't lust with long-denied love. It was genuine love.

As he sucked, he trailed his fingers across Peter's taint and the crack of his ass. His lover twitched and moaned beneath him, sometimes leaking precum into Jake's hungry mouth.

Reaching for a condom and lube, Jake worked quickly, loosening up Peter, making him comfortable, and then sliding his dick into Peter's hole. Peter groaned and Jake sighed. When he was buried to the hilt, he brought his upper body close to Peter and kissed him. He eased his hips back and forth, sliding his cock in and out, stimulating both of them, kissing Peter the entire time. Peter reached between their bodies and started stroking his dick.

Orgasm came quickly—far too quickly—and in the glorious aftermath, Jake rolled off Peter and cuddled him close, pulling the blanket up and covering them.

He nestled his face against the back of Peter's neck and breathed in the scent of his lover. *All of this is because of Grant*, he realized. The Scot had helped him open himself to his emotions, to his love, and act on it, to not be afraid of it. Though Grant had irritated him at first, the man had given Jake the greatest gift of all. Love.

"I love you, Peter," he whispered, dropping a gentle kiss on the back of Peter's neck.

"I love you too." And as he drifted off to sleep, he heard Peter murmur, "Welcome home, Jake."

About Cameron D. James

Cameron D. James is a life-long lover of books and telling stories…especially stories involving hot guys doing hot things. When not immersed in the pages of a novel, he can usually be found playing board games with friends or cuddling with one of his rescue cats. (Or, if the mood is right and he's a bit tipsy, playing board games with his cats and cuddling with his friends.)

After publishing nearly a hundred titles under a variety of pen names, many of which have become category bestsellers on Amazon or the now-defunct All Romance eBooks, Cameron started up Deep Desires Press, a publishing house for romance and erotica of all romantic pairings.

The best way to get in touch with Cameron is either by Twitter (@Cameron_D_James) or his website (http://www.camerondjames.com).

Books by Cameron D. James
Autumn Fire
Silent Hearts

Coming December 2018
New York Heat
A five-part serialized novel continuing Cameron D. James's best-selling and most-popular series, *Go-Go Boys of Club 21* and *Men In The Hot Room*! While some things stay the same, some things will never be the same again. This explosive and erotic novel is a must read!

Dear Reader,

Thank you for reading *Silent Hearts*! Many books thrive or perish based on reviews or a lack thereof. Please consider posting an honest review on the site you purchased this book from and/or on Goodreads. If you're new to writing reviews or wouldn't know how to write one, you could start by sharing what you found most enjoyable about this book.

Also, be sure to sign up for the Deep Desires Press newsletter. This is the best way to stay on top of new releases, meet the authors, and take advantage of coupons and deals. Please visit our website at www.deepdesirespress.com and look for the newsletter sign-up box at the bottom of the page.

Thanks again,
Deep Desires Press

WIN FREE BOOKS!

Our email newsletter is the best way to stay on top of all of our new releases, sales, and fantastic giveaways. All you have to do is visit deepdesirespress.com/newsletter and sign up today!

SUBSCRIBE TO OUR PODCAST!

Deep Desires Podcast releases monthly episodes where we talk to your favorite authors—or authors who will soon become your favorite! Find us on Apple Podcasts, Google Play Music, Stitcher, and our website (deepdesirespress.com/podcast/). Subscribe today!

Support the Deep Desires Podcast on Patreon and you can receive free ebooks every month! Find out more at patreon.com/deepdesirespodcast!

Don't Miss These Great Titles
from Deep Desires Press

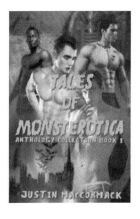

Tales of Monsterotica: Anthology Collection Book 1

Justin MacCormack

Classic monsters, classic gay sex. This hilariously hot book follows the madcap adventures of young Jonathan Woodcock and collects The Castle of Count Shagula, The Madness of Doctor Wankenstein, *and* The Curse of the Mummy's Wang *into one handy volume!*

Available now in paperback and ebook!

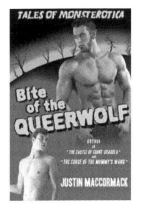

Bite of the Queerwolf
(Tales of Monsterotica #4)

Justin MacCormack

Having escaped Count Shagula, Doctor Wankenstein, and Pharaoh Gotabigun, Jonathan Woodcock is now in the hands of the leather-clad, dominating, powerful Queerwolf!

Available now in ebook!

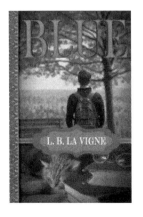

Blue
L.B. La Vigne

A wealthy businessman and rag-tag college student spark up an unlikely romance, but fear of commitment and skeletons from the past threaten their happy ever after.

Available now in paperback and ebook!

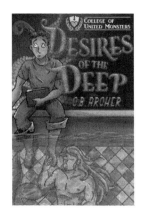

Desires of the Deep
(College of United Monsters #1)
C.B. Archer

What happens when you enroll in a monster college and end up stuck in underwater classes? Butt stuff. Butt stuff happens.

Available now in ebook!

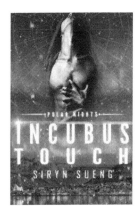

Incubus Touch
(Polar Nights #1)
Siryn Sueng

Sex with the dark incubus, Jakai, is far more erotic than Valyn ever imagined it could be. But when Valyn spots a terrifying figure in Jakai's yard, the peace in Tromsø, Norway begins to break apart—and their presence is just the beginning...

Available now in ebook!

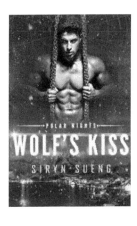

Wolf's Kiss
(Polar Nights #2)
Siryn Sueng

Nolan has heard werewolves love bondage and toys in the bedroom, but Halken brings more than just his kinky nature.

Available now in ebook!

Autumn Fire

Cameron D. James

True gay love is a fairy tale and the closet is comfier, until you meet the man of your dreams.

Available now in paperback and ebook!

The Line of Succession

Harry F. Rey

Andrew's dedicated his life to defending his secret lover, Prince James. But can their love survive his twin sister Princess Alexandra's schemes in the ensuing battle for the British crown?

Available now in paperback and ebook!

Made in the USA
Middletown, DE
19 July 2019